In recording the 50th Case of the redheaded private detective from Miami, Florida, and in celebration of his 25th year in print, Brett Halliday has diverged widely from the pattern set by 49 previous books.

Here, the emphasis is upon character and motivation rather than detection and deduction, and in so doing Mr. Halliday has produced his finest and most powerful novel.

Long-time fans of Michael Shayne will not be disappointed, and new readers will discover that an important dimension has been added to the routine novel of mystery and suspense.

MURDER AND THE WANTON BRIDE (1958)
FIT TO KILL (1958)
DATE WITH A DEAD MAN (1959)
TARGET: MIKE SHAYNE (1959)
DIE LIKE A DOG (1959)
MURDER TAKES NO HOLIDAY (1960)
DOLLS ARE DEADLY (1960)
THE HOMICIDAL VIRGIN (1960)
KILLERS FROM THE KEYS (1961)
MURDER IN HASTE (1961)
THE CARELESS CORPSE (1961)
PAY-OFF IN BLOOD (1962)
MURDER BY PROXY (1962)
NEVER KILL A CLIENT (1962)
TOO FRIENDLY, TOO DEAD (1963)
THE CORPSE THAT NEVER WAS (1963)
THE BODY CAME BACK (1963)
A REDHEAD FOR MIKE SHAYNE (1964)
SHOOT TO KILL (1964)

MICHAEL SHAYNE'S
50th CASE

BRETT HALLIDAY

A TORQUIL BOOK

Distributed by

DODD, MEAD & COMPANY

NEW YORK

Twenty-five years ago my first book
DIVIDEND ON DEATH
was dedicated as follows:

For MONTY
because he likes this story.

Today, I am proud to dedicate my 50th book to:
Rutherford G. Montgomery
and a friendship that has endured thirty years.

1

It was a little after three o'clock in the afternoon and Marvin Blake sat alone in his hotel room in Miami looking forward to the evening that lay ahead of him with a certain amount of distaste. Perhaps there was a bit of dread mixed with his distaste, although that is a strong word for what Marvin was feeling.

Certainly, he wasn't looking forward to the night with any eagerness or anticipation. Thus far, he conceded to himself, it had been a good convention. This was the final day of it and he had just come back to his room after attending the last formal meeting on the agenda.

Tonight was the night for making whoopee. The night for cutting loose from all restraints and raising hell just for the pure fun of it. The night, in fact, that most of the delegates looked forward to with enthusiastic anticipation. The reason most of them had come to the convention in the first place.

Many of the delegates, of course, had been whooping things up ever since they had been in the city. But tonight was the big one. Tomorrow they would all disperse and go back to their humdrum lives at home. Most of them would go back to small communities like Sunray Beach, which was Marvin Blake's home-town where they were solid and respected citizens, members of the Chamber of Commerce and the Elks or the Lions, good husbands and fathers, sober and dependable taxpayers who helped to keep the National Economy in gear.

But tonight they were going to be anonymous John and Bill and Henry and Mike, according to the labels pinned to their lapels. Tonight they were going to be on the town, and they were all set to raise merry hell because they couldn't raise hell at home without everyone in town knowing about it. Because they were just adolescents at heart and never really had grown up, and were all loaded down with frustrations and repressions and sublimations that called for some sort of outlet when the opportunity arose.

And Blake knew he would have to be "Marv" along with the rest of the boys. He would be expected to drink too much, and laugh too often and too loudly, and kiss the party girls who would be provided, and try to get some sort of erotic thrill out of the pornographic movie that would be shown in the Grand Ballroom as a fun-making climax to the four-day convention.

Marvin Blake didn't like to drink too much, but he

glumly knew that he would do so tonight. He knew he'd start out promising himself he'd have only two or three, and he'd gulp down those two or three, and then another and just another, and pretty soon he'd be snatching a glass from every loaded tray that went by and things would begin to get a little blurred . . . and there he'd be!

And the next morning he'd wake up (alone in his own hotel room if he was lucky) with a head as big as a balloon and an awful taste in his mouth and little men hammering on the inside of his skull with croquet mallets, and wondering why in hell he had done it, and just what *had* happened after he passed out.

And if he wasn't lucky, there'd maybe be a floosie in bed with him when he woke up, or lipstick stains on the pillow and the pervasive stink of perfume and passion in the room. And then, along with the hangover there'd be a dreadful feeling of guilt and remorse that he'd carry away with him and take back home and have to learn to live with for all the years to come.

He shuddered with revulsion at his imaginings, and tried to put them away from him. Up to this point it had been a darned good convention. He was glad he had come even if the trip had turned out a little more expensive than he had anticipated. Ellie had been right when she insisted that he must attend it. A man does need to get away from home once in a while. Does him good to get together with other fellows and talk business and how the last sales campaign went, and why it didn't go better, and what the economic outlook for the coming year is and things like that. It broadens a man's horizons and makes him realize that all over the country other fellows face the same sort of problems he faces.

Yes, Marvin was glad he had come, all right. He told himself that Ellie had been wonderful the way she insisted he just take the money out of the savings account and go, even if he had felt he couldn't afford it. Just thinking about Ellie made him feel warm and good. She had insisted that she could get along fine without him for just four days. My goodness! why shouldn't she? Didn't she get along all right every day with him away at the office?

Thinking about Ellie brought a twinge of guilt feelings to Marvin. Why had he fooled around with that redhead up in Tom Connors' suite last night? Well, he asked himself angrily, why *had* he? She was common and coarse, and nothing but a damned gold-digger. Anyone could see that with half an eye. Why does a man do damn fool things like that when he has a wife like Ellie waiting for him at home? And a sweet little daughter like Sissy. Both of them believing you're the salt of the earth and that you're completely to be trusted away from home.

It hadn't been much, of course. Not anything, really. He hadn't actually kissed her, but you can't pull away and make a scene in front of the other fellows when a pretty girl wants to kiss you. Not unless you want to get laughed at.

The redhead was part of his worry about the coming evening. The last thing she'd whispered in his ear before the party broke up at midnight was that she was looking forward to getting better acquainted tonight.

Marvin Blake didn't *want* to see the redhead again. He

didn't even like her because, my goodness, how can a man like a girl like that if he's married to someone like Ellie?

Thinking about Ellie made Marvin want to telephone her. It would be reassuring and good to hear her warm throaty voice over the telephone telling him that Sissy was perfectly wonderful although she missed her Daddy dreadfully, and that they were absolutely all right at home and hoped he was having fun in Miami.

But Ellie had made him promise not to telephone her from Miami. She said that after they had been married eight years it was just foolish to waste money on long distance calls. She had made him promise to send her a ten-word telegram the minute he arrived safely at the hotel, and then not to waste money phoning her. "You go out and spend that extra money on cocktails," she'd told him with a laugh. "Goodness knows, you deserve an outing every year or so. You just have a real good time in Miami and don't you worry about Sissy and me."

So he knew he'd better not telephone her. A long distance call would just frighten her and he'd have a hard time explaining that he'd just called on an impulse because he wanted to hear her voice. She'd remind him that he was coming home the next day anyhow, and she'd wonder why he couldn't wait one more day.

He could get out of the shindig tonight, of course. He could slip out of the hotel before five o'clock and go some place to have dinner alone and then maybe to a movie. He knew very well that no one would really miss him. Not even the redhead. He knew that well enough. She would find plenty of other men to cuddle up to. Oh, some of the fellows might wonder where Marv was, but not for long. Not after four or five drinks. And it wasn't as though it would do him any good in a business way. He had already made all his contacts and got all the real good out of the convention that there was. Tonight was strictly for fun.

For fun! He sat disconsolately in his hotel room and shuddered as he envisioned the main event in the Grand Ballroom after the delegates had lapped up all the liquor they could hold and were ready for it.

He wondered where they got hold of movies like the one that was promised for tonight. Who makes them, and who really wants to see them? Well, he had to reluctantly admit to himself that apparently a majority of the delegates to conventions such as this one *do* enjoy looking at that sort of smut. He'd been to other conventions in the past and seen how they crowded in.

But why, he wondered. In the name of God, *why?* Taken all in all, he and his fellow delegates were a fairly representative sector of the American way of life. What sort of kick does a decent guy get out of sitting in the darkness with a lot of other men and watching that kind of stuff on a screen?

Then he wondered if he was being a bit of a prude. He didn't think of himself as prudish. Actually, he was all for sex. He thought sex was wonderful. He was thirty-five years old and normally masculine, and he defied any man to get more pleasure out of sex than he did.

With the *right* woman . . . at the *right* time.

But he didn't anticipate any sexual pleasure from sitting through the sort of display that was slated for the delegates tonight. He considered it abnormal. A perverted sort of thing. But he knew that if he dared express his opinion out loud he would be hooted at all over the place by his friends. It would be he who would be considered abnormal. Somehow or other, he decided, it has come to be considered one of the marks of robust American masculinity to enjoy such exhibitions.

And he wondered vaguely how that had come about. Had it always been so, or was it one of the newer and more unpleasant aspects of modern living? And he wondered if American males were different, or if it was the same throughout the world when men go out together and don't have to answer to their womenfolk.

Anyhow, he supposed he'd better attend the thing. A man has to go along and pretend to be one of the boys. And suddenly he caught himself wondering how many of the others felt about the coming evening as he did. It was interesting to speculate on that. How many of the others were simply going along to be Good Sports? If a secret poll were taken and the real truth arrived at, he wondered how many others would prefer to have the convention end right now so they could go on home to their wives and children without spending this final night in Miami.

While he was asking himself that question without getting any answer, he caught himself studying a printed warning lying on the table beside him. In large black letters, it said:

CHECK-OUT TIME AT THIS HOTEL IS 4 P. M.

He looked at his watch without quite knowing why he

did so. It was 3:22. In thirty-eight minutes the official hotel day would end and another would start. Another twelve dollars charged to him for the room he was sitting in.

The whole trip, darn it, had been quite expensive. Like twelve dollars for a dinky little hotel room. And that was a special rate for the delegates, of course. You could get a larger and much nicer room at the new Sunray Motel for eight dollars a night. And that was the regular rate. And everything else in Miami was more expensive in proportion. Breakfast cost from seventy-five cents to two dollars, depending on how hungry you were, with an extra service charge and a tip if you felt lazy and had it brought to your room. Cocktails were a dollar each in the Starroom downstairs, and dinners from three dollars up.

He hadn't kept track of every penny he'd spent in four days, but he knew it was a little over thirty-five dollars in cash on top of his hotel bill. Plus the chits he had signed. Say, forty-five dollars at least. And in exactly another thirty-eight minutes there would be another twelve-dollar room charge added to that. More than eighty dollars, at least, and by the time the evening was over and next morning's breakfast it would be a hundred dollars easily.

That wasn't so bad, actually, Marvin reassured himself. He had warned Ellie in the beginning that the trip was likely to cost at least a hundred dollars. She insisted that they could afford it. And she had made him bring along another fifty dollars in cash for "extras."

So he had plenty of money, all right. But it bothered Marvin to spend so much on himself and have nothing to show for it. Oh, he had a small present for Sissy in his bag.

A father can't go away to the city on a four-day trip and not take a present back to his six-year-old daughter. Not if he wanted her to go on thinking he was the most wonderful Daddy in the world. And he had bought a nice box of chocolates for Ellie. Just something so she would know he had thought about her while he was away.

But he did wish he felt he could afford to buy the earrings he had seen in the little gift shop next door to the hotel. They were really beautiful, and just right for Ellie. They were large and shaped like flowers, each petal inlaid with mother-of-pearl and rimmed with gold. The mother-of-pearl caught the light and reflected it in iridescent colors. Sitting there in the hotel room, he could visualize the earrings fastened to Ellie's pretty ear lobes, contrasting with her thick, black hair which curled around her face and formed the perfect background for the gleaming mother-of-pearl. They would be for the times she wore an evening gown. That was only on special occasions, but those earrings were just what she needed to add the finishing touch for those occasions.

He was tempted again as he sat there and thought about the earrings. But he knew he'd better not buy them. Ellie would love them all right, but she'd know right away that they must have been awfully expensive and she'd never let up on him until she found out how much they had cost. And when she did find out she would more than likely put them away regretfully in a drawer because she'd feel guilty wearing anything that cost that much . . . and so what would be the good of his splurging on them?

Twelve dollars for one night in a hotel room, he thought,

and the earrings that were too expensive to buy for Ellie only cost twenty-eight dollars.

Then the brilliant idea came to him, and he sat upright excitedly while he thought it all out. Ellie wouldn't mind his spending so much on a gift for her if he could prove that he had saved it somewhere else. A minute ago he had figured he must be out about eighty dollars already on the trip. Not counting his railroad ticket. And his room and everything tonight would run another twenty at the very least.

But it wasn't four o'clock yet. It was still almost thirty minutes before another hotel day started. And there he was, sitting around dreading the evening to come. An evening that was going to cost him twenty dollars or even more! And he couldn't afford to spend twenty-eight dollars for a wonderful present for Ellie that would cause her eyes to light up and get all warm and loving when she saw them.

The heck he couldn't! Wasn't there a late afternoon train to Sunray Beach? Leaving Miami about six o'clock and getting in between ten and eleven?

He got up swiftly and went to the closet where he dragged out his suitcase and got out the railroad timetable. He was right. There was a train leaving at 6:32 and arriving at Sunray Beach at 10:20. There was a little g in front of it and he had to check the list of symbols to see what a "g" meant.

Stops only to discharge passengers.

Well, that was all right. He had a return ticket to Sunray so they'd have to stop and let him off. It was pretty late to be getting home and there wouldn't be any taxi at the station because that train didn't stop very often. Probably no one else getting off either who could give him a ride home.

Of course, he thought, he could telephone Ellie to tell her he was coming, and she'd be at the station to meet him. She didn't expect him back until tomorrow afternoon, and he thought to himself how happy her voice would be if he told her he was homesick for her and Sissy and was coming home tonight instead. She'd be there at the station to meet him, all right. And with Sissy, too. For a special occasion like this, Ellie was the kind of wife and mother who'd break all the rules and keep Sissy up for the fun of going to the station and meeting her Daddy.

He started across the room to the telephone to call Ellie, and he picked it up before hesitating and putting it down again. He wasn't going to do it. How much more fun to surprise her! It was only six blocks from the station to their house. He could walk it easily, and his suitcase wasn't very heavy.

He knew he was going to do it, all through the couple of minutes that he stood in the middle of the hotel room and tried to think up some good reason for staying the night in Miami instead.

There weren't any good reasons. He reminded himself that he had even contemplated slipping out and going to a movie by himself. Why pay the hotel twelve dollars for the privilege of seeing a movie? He could go to the movies at home with Ellie.

He didn't have to tell anyone he was checking out. If any of the fellows did see him in the lobby and asked any questions, he could tell them he'd had a message from home.

His little girl was ill. An emergency. And anyway, why did he have to explain himself to a bunch of drunks?

He'd check out right away and have plenty of time to pick up the earrings for Ellie. Then he'd go on to the station and have time to stop on the way at some cheap restaurant and get some supper before boarding the train, and avoid the high prices they charged in the dining car.

And if he was hungry again by the time he got home to Sunray Beach, Ellie could fix him a snack. It would be fun slipping down to the kitchen about midnight with Sissy sound asleep, and maybe both of them having a drink together first, and then some scrambled eggs or something.

Ellie with her black hair braided and wound around her head like she did at night, and her black eyes sparkling with excitement and happiness on account of the earrings and about his coming home unexpectedly and ahead of time.

Ellie in her bare feet and her pink nightgown, and the clean, little-girl look of her unrouged face just wakened out of a sound sleep.

Suddenly he wanted to see Ellie real bad. It was as though it had been years since he had seen her. He picked up the telephone and asked for the cashier's desk, and said: "This is Mr. Blake in Six-ten. I'm checking out at once. Please get my bill ready and send a boy up to get my bag."

Then he hung up and started tossing things into his suitcase so it'd be ready when the boy came for it.

2

Marvin Blake was waiting impatiently at the cashier's wicket for change from the three twenties he had shoved across the counter with his room-key when he heard his name being called loudly from behind him. He turned his head and saw Hal Jackson and Joe Wallis weaving across the lobby with their arms linked together, grinning widely and somewhat fatuously.

They were partners in an automobile agency in Moonray Beach, about thirty miles south of Sunray on the coast, and they were competitors of Marvin's. They were both good fellows and he had known them for years, and he knew they would demand explanations from him if they realized he was checking out before the end of the convention.

They were both pretty well plastered at this early hour

in the afternoon, bumping into people and making loud remarks to each other about the pretty women they passed. Not lewd remarks or really offensive. Just what they considered good clean fun, and everyone who saw their delegate badges just smiled or shrugged their shoulders and passed them off for just what they were—a couple of typical small-town businessmen winding up a four-day convention away from home.

They had already seen Marvin standing there and he knew he couldn't avoid an encounter with them, so he was relieved when the cashier pushed back a receipted hotel bill with some one-dollar bills and silver and he was able to slide it into his pocket before they reached him, so they didn't realize he had just paid his bill.

"Marv, old man!" Hal Jackson bellowed, pounding him on the shoulder and almost falling flat on his face in the process. "Whatcha doing here, huh? Run out of mazuma already and stocking up for the night? Trying to talk this sucker into cashing a check for you? Tell you what, Mister." He leaned past Marvin, supporting himself with an arm about his shoulder, and blew whiskey-laden fumes in the cashier's face. "Take a tip from me and don't cash any checks signed Marvin Blake. A dead-beat, that's what he is. A no-good dead-beat from Sunray Beach."

The cashier smiled as politely as he could and pointedly looked past them at some other people waiting to check out, and Marvin pulled the two men aside and Joe Wallis suggested they all go into the bar for a drink, and where did Marv dig up that redhead he had seen him with last night?

And Hal laughed uproariously and nudged Marvin in the ribs and warned him in a loud voice: "Wait'll we see Ellie again, by golly. Just you wait, Marv old boy. Will we give Ellie an earful?"

"That is," put in Joe with a broad wink, "unless Marv agrees to share the redhead with his old pals tonight. How's about it, Marv? That's all we ask from a buddy. Just an ittsy-bittsy share. Anybody can see with half an eye that redhead's got plenty of stuff to spread around."

Blushing, Marvin Blake shushed them as best he could, conscious of the knowing and superior smiles of strangers around them, and he finally persuaded them to go upstairs to their fourth floor suite by telling them he had a date to meet the redhead and would bring her right up to their suite for a drink and to get acquainted.

The bellboy was waiting with his suitcase near the door, and Marvin waited until Hal and Joe disappeared inside an elevator before he tipped the boy and took his bag and slipped out of the hotel without being noticed by anyone else.

He stepped quickly into the gift shop next door and set his suitcase inside and asked the lady clerk to let him see the pair of earrings displayed in the window.

She had another pair just like them in stock, and she set them out on the counter in a square white box with cushiony velvet underneath them.

Close up, they were even prettier than they had looked in the window, and Marvin told her he'd take them and would she wrap them as a gift, please.

She said she would be pleased to, and asked if he would

care to enclose a card. He hadn't thought about that, but as soon as she mentioned it he knew Ellie would be pleased if he did, so he asked if she had one he could write on.

She had an assortment to choose from, and wanted to know if it was for an anniversary or birthday gift, or what, and Marvin felt silly when he had to admit it wasn't any special occasion but just for his wife as a souvenir of his trip to Miami.

She gave him a plain white card with an envelope to match, and Marvin puckered up his forehead and thought hard for a moment, and then wrote firmly: "For my very best girl with love from Marvin." He sealed it in the envelope and the saleslady wrapped the box up in green and white striped paper and tied it with a white ribbon, and he paid her for it happily.

He slid the box into his inside breast pocket and it pressed against his chest and felt warm and good there as he picked up his suitcase and strode out onto the street again. It was less than a dozen blocks to the railway station and he had lots of time to kill before his train left, so he decided to walk and save taxi fare.

Actually, when he looked at his hotel bill and the change he'd received from the cashier he had discovered that the bill was several dollars more than he had anticipated, and he tried to think back as he walked down the street with his suitcase to see how he had mentally miscalculated what the bill would be.

Three days made thirty-six dollars for the room, but he hadn't thought to add the tax onto that. There had been three breakfasts for an average of about a dollar each, and three lunches for four-fifty or maybe five dollars. But there was only one dinner charged on the hotel bill. That was Tuesday night. But now he remembered that Tom Brent and a girl had stopped by his table at dinner and he'd ordered them a drink and had one himself to keep them company, and so that ran the dinner bill pretty high.

Oh, he was sure the hotel hadn't made a mistake, even if the total bill was fifty-four dollars and sixteen cents, and he couldn't help grinning as he walked along and thought how he had practically beat them out of another twelve bucks by checking out at four o'clock.

He watched out for a quiet, cheap-looking restaurant as he neared the station, and he found one that looked clean and had a menu in the window that featured Superburgers with all the fixings for 89c. He had a good meal there sitting at the counter and topping it off with a piece of apple pie and a cup of coffee which he dawdled over as long as he could make it last, and then he went on to the station and found his train waiting to be boarded, and he bought a *News* and got on and found a good seat in a smoker before the cars began to fill up.

My, but he felt good and sort of smug sitting there waiting for the train to pull out and take him back to Sunray Beach and to Ellie . . . and Sissy. The square box kept pressing against his chest under his coat so he was conscious of it, and he kept thinking about how Ellie's face would light up when he handed it to her and she opened it up. He'd do it that night, he decided happily. He wouldn't put it off until the next day. There would still be the box of chocolates that he could give her when he gave Sissy her present next morning, but the earrings were special.

They were for this first night.

Then the train started and he sat back comfortably in his seat and thought about all the others still back at the hotel, Hal and Joe and all the rest of them, getting drunk tonight and watching a smutty movie and waking up with God-awful hangovers the next morning, and he felt sorry for them because most of them didn't have a wife like Ellie to go home to.

He knew Hal and Joe didn't, for instance. He'd met both their wives at parties in the past, and had to admit to himself that if he were married to either one of them he wouldn't feel like hurrying home either. No, sir. He knew deep down inside himself that he'd be staying in Miami until the last dog was hung and get as soused as a field hand on Saturday night and do his best to forget about the little woman waiting for him at home.

Little woman! He had to grin at that expression as he thought about Hal's and Joe's wives. Mrs. Jackson was tall and horse-faced. She looked years older than Hal, and a lot of people said that the only reason he ever married her was because she had money to put into the business which made up enough for him to go into partnership with Joe Wallis.

Well, he told himself indulgently, you pay for whatever you get in this world. Hal had got himself half-share in a thriving automobile agency, but he had to live with that woman to pay for it. It was difficult to imagine Hal and his wife in bed together. She'd be bony, and she wouldn't like it, Marvin thought. She'd consider it was her duty, and she probably rationed poor old Hal to so many times a week.

Or so many times a month was more like it.

Joe Wallis' wife was different, but just as bad, it seemed to Marvin, in her own way. Suzy, he remembered her name was. Round-faced and with fluffy hair that Ellie declared was dyed. And a flirt if there ever was one. Ellie often said she didn't see how Joe could stand the way she acted, and Marvin had to agree that he didn't either. Not that she ever *did* anything, likely. He'd told Ellie that, right out, and she'd sort of agreed with him, though she still had certain reservations on the subject.

But she would insist on rubbing up against a man when she danced with him at a party, and she'd sort of accidentally let her knee touch his if they sat at table together, and little things like that. And she had a way of getting a man to go out in the kitchen with her alone at their house to help make drinks at a party, and she'd drop remarks that had double meanings if you looked for them. And kissing you behind the kitchen door if you'd had enough to drink and didn't push her away in disgust.

That had happened to Marvin once several years ago, and he still remembered it vividly and felt a little squirmish inside when he did. He never would forget the look on Ellie's face that night when he and Suzy finally came back out of the kitchen with a tray of drinks, but she didn't say a word to him about it right then. However, they were hardly out of the house and started for home when Ellie had lit into him, demanding to know just *what* he and Suzy had been doing alone in the kitchen all that time.

He hadn't dared tell Ellie the truth. How Suzy had caught him unaware and pushed her body against him and lifted up her face with parted lips, and how something had come over him and he'd kissed her. He was heartily ashamed of the incident mostly because he had really enjoyed it while it was going on.

He had puzzled about that for a long time afterward. He just couldn't understand how a supposedly decent man could enjoy kissing another woman while he was very much in love with his wife at the same time. That is, really *like* it, the way he had with Suzy that night. He knew, as honestly as he knew anything, that he didn't really *want* another woman sexually. Yet, for a minute or so he *had* wanted Suzy. He had finally decided it had been too much liquor that was to blame. And after that he had been careful not to take more than two or three drinks in any one evening, particularly if Suzy was around.

At home alone with Ellie it was different, of course. Neither one of them were prudes about drinking or sex. Several times since they'd been married they had cut loose in the evening and got good and tight together at home, and the results had been wonderful. They had done all sorts of wild and crazy things in bed, things that a lot of people would probably call indecent, but neither of them had been the slightest bit ashamed of it the next day when they sobered up and remembered what they had done. They had actually talked about it, and agreed that it was a good thing for married couples to do once in awhile, and Marvin felt sure that if more people did it there'd be less fooling around outside the home.

It was dark outside by the time he had finished these thoughts, and the fast train was rolling smoothly up the coastline toward Sunray Beach and Ellie, and Marvin felt warm and good and smugly self-righteous when he thought about what the other delegates were doing back in that Miami hotel. The car wasn't crowded and he had a whole seat to himself, and he opened the newspaper and glanced at the headlines, and he was dozing off a little when the conductor tapped him on the shoulder for his ticket.

He gave it to him and chuckled as he said, "Sorry to cause you so much trouble, but I guess you're going to have to stop and let me off at Sunray."

The conductor punched the ticket with a smile and assured him they didn't mind stopping, and that if Marvin wanted to take a little snooze to go on and do it because the conductor would promise to wake him up personally in time to get off.

Marvin thought that was nice of him, and he did doze off some more, and the next thing he knew the conductor was tapping him on the shoulder again and the train was beginning to slow down. Marvin yawned and looked out the window and saw the big neon sign of the Sunray Motel sliding past, and suddenly he was wide awake and excited to be getting home. He got his suitcase down from the overhead rack and went back and was waiting in the vestibule for the door to be opened when the train ground to a protesting stop.

He stepped down onto the cindered walk quickly, and there was bright starlight and a little sickle of moon in the sky, and he breathed the good fresh air deeply into his lungs and it smelled good after sitting in the smoker so long.

The train just barely came to a full stop, then picked up

speed and glided away and he stood there and watched the lighted cars slide past until there were just the twin red lights receding and fading into the night.

Just as Marvin had anticipated, he was the only passenger to get off the train. There was a dim light inside the waiting room and he walked up there and looked in, but wasn't surprised to find it empty. It was well past ten o'clock and that meant that all the business places were closed up tight and all the residents were asleep or at least snugly inside their own homes.

He walked around the waiting room and there wasn't any taxi, of course, but he didn't mind at all. The six-block walk to his home was exactly what he needed to clean the city air out of his lungs.

Pleasant Street, leading away from the depot, was tree-lined and lighted with street lamps at every second corner. Marvin walked along it briskly, glancing pleasurably at the well-kept lawns and houses as he passed them. The Burkes and the Chadwicks and the Evanses. Solid, substantial homes with neat, palm-shaded driveways and carefully-tended tropical shrubbery in the yards. All of them dark, now, except Dr. Higgens' three-story house on the corner of Pleasant Street and Starfish Lane. There was a dim light downstairs as Marvin went by, and another in a third floor bedroom.

He wondered if someone in town were sick and hoped it wasn't serious, and then he quickened his pace just a little as he recalled that he had been away from home four whole days without any word, and that Sissy had sniffled a little the morning he left and Ellie had said she thought she'd better keep her home from first grade for a day or so just in case it did develop into something the other children could catch.

He knew it was foolish to let a night light in the doctor's house worry him about Sissy, but he pushed on a little faster anyway, turning into Lily Lane three blocks from the depot. It was a winding street in a newer part of town, and all the houses were modern and had larger grounds than in the older part of Sunray, each with private driveways leading up to secluded houses that were set well apart from their neighbors.

As he climbed the slope toward his own driveway, Marvin thought pleasurably how it would be when he got home. He had his latch-key, of course. Ellie and Sissy would be sleeping soundly in the adjoining bedrooms upstairs and he wouldn't have to wake them to get in. They both slept very soundly and they weren't expecting him.

He'd leave his suitcase downstairs in the hall, he decided, and go into the kitchen quietly and get two glasses and the bottle of imported cognac that Ellie kept pushed back on the top shelf for special occasions.

Then he'd go upstairs on tiptoe and into the big front bedroom where starlight would be shining through the two open windows and making enough light to show Ellie lying asleep in bed.

She mostly slept on her left side with her cheek pillowed on her arm, and the cover was always slipping down from her right shoulder and leaving it bare.

He'd kneel beside the bed, he thought happily, and waken her with a kiss on her bare shoulder, and she'd lift up her head sleepily, not quite knowing who it was or what was happening, and then he'd kiss her hard on the mouth and she'd come fully awake and cling to him and kiss him back.

Then he thought of a better way. He'd close the door through the bathroom into Sissy's room and lock it first, and then he'd undress without turning on a light and go around the bed and slip under the covers on the other side of Ellie without waking her.

There was a sort of good animal smell that came from Ellie's body when she was asleep. Different from when she was awake. Marvin always thought of it as a sensuous smell. He often waked up in the night with her lying close beside him, and he'd smell her smell and snuggle a little closer to her and bury his face under the covers against her back and breathe in deeply of the lovely fragrance that was his wife.

And almost always it had a powerful stimulating effect on him. He didn't intend to waken her and he tried not to, but generally she'd seem to sense how he was feeling, even in her sleep, and she'd turn slowly and languidly to him, and sometimes he thought she didn't even wake up fully even when it was all over, but he didn't mind that because she was loving and willing whenever he wanted to, and he considered that all a man should want from his wife in the middle of the night.

He reached their driveway and it wound up between a double row of hibiscus to the front of the house which he could scarcely see from the street. He followed the drive up and around, and stopped suddenly when he saw a dim light behind drawn shades in the front bedroom window.

He saw at once that it wasn't in Sissy's room, and he stopped being frightened. It wasn't actually very late and there was no reason in the world why Ellie shouldn't still be awake and up. She might even be reading in bed, which was something she had given up after she married Marvin.

He went on up the drive to the last turn where he could see the lower front of the house clearly, and there he stopped again.

There was a car standing in the darkness under the *porte cochère* directly in front. For a brief moment he was irritated by the sight of it there. Ellie knew how he felt about automobiles. He always said that garages were built to protect cars from the damp night air, and he never allowed one to sit out at night.

He stepped closer and his irritation vanished and turned into something else. It was neither his sedan nor Ellie's coupé that stood in front of his house. It was a convertible with the top down and with lots of bright chrome.

He took two more hesitant steps forward and stopped again. He recognized the convertible. It belonged to Harry. Harry Wilsson. One of their closest neighbors, and Marvin's best friend in Sunray.

3

He stood there in the night, petrified and disbelieving, staring at the convertible parked in front of his house, knowing there must be some mistake.

Oh, it was Harry Wilsson's car all right. There was no mistake about that. There were only two or three convertibles in Sunray, and Marvin had sold this one to Harry Wilsson himself about two months ago. They had argued together good-naturedly about the trade-in value of the Dodge sedan that Harry was turning in on it, and Marvin had ended up by giving his good friend a deal that had left him with almost no profit on the transaction.

But he knew there must be some mistake about its being there at his house tonight. That is, some simple and reasonable explanation. His first thought was that Harry and Minerva had dropped over to spend the evening with Ellie and cheer her up on the last night her husband was away from home. That was a perfectly natural thing to think. The couples visited back and forth together quite informally all the time.

But why was the light on only in Ellie's bedroom and the rest of the house dark?

Well, he thought, maybe it was just Minerva who had come over for the evening. It was perfectly natural that the two women might have taken a drink up to the bedroom to relax and have a session of female talk.

But why hadn't Minerva driven her own Plymouth coupé if that was it? Harry was funny and very possessive about his new convertible. He didn't trust Minerva to drive it because she was a careless driver and was always scraping a fender or smashing a headlight in minor accidents. Marvin distinctly remembered an on-the-surface laughing but under-the-surface acrimonious discussion about that very thing between the Wilssons the night after Harry brought his new convertible home.

So there had to be some other answer.

What was it?

Suppose Sissy were sick and the Wilssons had come over to help. Maybe that was why they were all upstairs in the bedroom and the rest of the house dark.

But there was no light showing in Sissy's bedroom. Marvin Blake stood in his own driveway not more than thirty feet from the house staring up at the shaded bedroom window and straining his ears to pick up some sound. But the house was shrouded in utter silence. And it was awful funny to see the shades drawn at the bedroom window, too. It was quite a warm night and their house was so secluded that no passerby could look into the upstairs rooms, and Marvin couldn't remember those shades ever being drawn at night before.

He stood there looking helplessly up at the shaded windows and hearing no sound from within the bedroom. All he had to do was walk up to his own front door and put his key in the latch and open the door and shout up the stairs, "Yoo-hoo, Ellie. It's me. Marv. I'm home."

That's all he had to do. Simplest thing in the world. So, why didn't he *do* it? Why did he stand there like a ninny, transfixed, his heart beating queerly, his mouth dry and his stomach churning?

Because he thought for a moment there was anything wrong inside his house? Because he was afraid of what might be going on behind the drawn shades in that bedroom? Because he even remotely suspected the possibility that Ellie and Harry . . . that Ellie and Harry might . . .?

Oh God, *no*! He shook himself like a man emerging from a trance. What a foul and nasty mind he had! To even *think* that of Ellie. Or Harry either. Harry was his best and most-trusted friend. He'd no more think of a thing like that than. . . .

And Ellie! Good God, he *knew* Ellie, didn't he? She was his wife. She was Sissy's mother. She loved him. She'd no more do that with Harry than she'd. . . .

Well, all he had to do was walk in the front door and prove that he had a foul and nasty mind.

That was all he had to do.

But suppose . . .?

If he did walk in the front door the stairs leading up would be right in front of him and there'd be no back way out for Harry if he was upstairs with Ellie. The two of them would be cornered if he walked in the front door.

He had a revolver. It was loaded and ready to shoot and it rested handy in the top drawer of the bureau right there in the hall.

He could go in quietly and get the gun out and then go upstairs and see what was what.

Suppose Harry were there with Ellie?

He could shoot them both. It was the unwritten law that he could.

Not Ellie!

Yes, Ellie, too. Didn't his manhood demand it?

Damn his manhood and the unwritten law! What *was* he thinking about? Because it wasn't so. None of it was so. There was some other explanation for Harry's car being there and a single light on in the bedroom behind drawn shades and the silence. All he had to do was walk in the front door and find out what the real explanation was.

He couldn't walk in the front door.

He didn't believe any of it for a moment, but he couldn't put it to the test.

Because, supposing it were so? What would he do then?

He couldn't be an outraged husband and start shooting to protest his honor. It simply wasn't in him to do that.

There was the detached and dignified approach, of course. Something like: "Sorry to break in on you two like this, but I simply didn't know how it was with you. It's all *right*, Ellie. If you prefer Harry to me, why should I stand in your way? I'll expect custody of Sissy, of course. And I'll expect you to do the honorable thing by her, Harry old boy."

No. Marvin knew that wasn't for him either. So, what *could* he do?

God, he thought helplessly, if only he hadn't come home tonight. If only there'd been some warning. If only he had *known* he shouldn't come unexpectedly and had telephoned Ellie from Miami.

Well, he could turn away now and slip back to the station without being seen and catch that late train back to Miami, and then come back tomorrow afternoon on schedule . . . and he would never need to know.

Could he do that? Could he stand to go on living with Ellie without knowing? He could never ask Ellie. He could never admit to her that he had come home tonight and seen Harry's car outside and turned away because he suspected something bad.

No, he couldn't go on living without knowing for sure. First, he had to know what the truth was. After that he could decide what to do, how to live with it.

He shrank back into the shadow of the hibiscus hedge and set his suitcase down very carefully so as to make no sound. Then he lowered his weight down on it and buried his face in his hands.

He told himself angrily that he had a dirty mind. If he trusted Ellie at all . . . if their marriage vows meant anything to him . . . he would go boldly up to the front door and at least ring the bell and give Ellie a chance to come down and explain the situation.

Ellie deserved that much trust. Where was his faith in her? Didn't he *know* she loved him? He was a lousy bastard to let himself suspect for one single moment that Ellie would do anything wrong. He was surely going to hate himself when it all came out in a simple and innocent explanation.

All right, he told himself fiercely, so he would hate himself. But he knew he would hate himself more if he forced the issue and it turned out there was no innocent explanation. That would mean he would have to leave Ellie. No man and wife can go on living together after one has been caught committing adultery.

Why not, he asked himself miserably. Why did it matter so much? Would Ellie be a different person just because she was in bed with another man tonight? Would there be any physical change in her? Wouldn't she still be the same Ellie he had loved for ten years? The mother of his child. Would one physical contact with Harry Wilsson change Ellie so much that he couldn't live with her afterward?

And he answered himself with an emphatic NO to all those questions. Yet he knew there *would* be a disastrous change in their relationship if he walked into the house and caught her in bed with Harry. All three of them would have to react to that. Marvin did not know why this was so. He didn't understand why people *had* to react to a situation like that. But he knew that each of them would. He knew that three or four or five lives would inevitably be smashed into little pieces if he went into the house and found his wife and Harry Wilsson together intimately.

He couldn't take a chance on doing that to himself and Ellie and Sissy. He couldn't, God help him, do that to

Harry and Minerva. He could not take the risk of going inside his own house.

But he could not, either, go away from the house without knowing for certain. Even though, God knew, he wanted to go away from there.

But that, he could not do.

Yet all the time he did not actually believe in his heart that there was anything wrong. He knew he was getting it all wrong and that there must be an innocent explanation. That is, he *tried* to know. He willed himself to know. But the inner knowledge was not strong enough to force him to take the ultimate step.

He knew it was a weak thing to do, and he despised himself for his own weakness as he crouched there in the shadows with his hands over his face and did not dare to enter his own home.

But he wondered how many other husbands would have been stronger than he? Oh, he knew a lot of men who would have dashed into the house at the first intimation that his wife might be unfaithful, waving a gun and shouting that his honor must be avenged. But in his heart Marvin believed that sort of man was in the minority.

What does a man's honor have to do with it, he asked himself. It is his life that is at stake. His future. Everything that he holds dear. Should a man smash that up in one instant of jealous rage which he will regret the rest of his life?

Oh, he was jealous all right. He was writhing and aching and seared with jealousy. He simply could not allow himself to visualize Ellie and Harry in bed together. It was too monstrous. If he just didn't have to *see* it with his own eyes.

So he stayed there seated on his suitcase in the shadows and he waited. And kept his face buried in his hands so he could not look up to the dim light in the bedroom. Their bedroom. Ellie's and his. The bedchamber he had brought her to as a bride and where her maidenhead had been broken. Where Sissy had been conceived.

He did not know how long he sat there. It seemed like many hours, but he knew it was probably less than one. He did not know what caused him to finally lift his head and gaze dully at the house again, but just as he did so he saw a light come on inside the frosted glass upper portion of the front door. That meant to him that the stairway light had been switched on from above and that someone was coming down the stairs.

The bedroom light remained lit.

He remained hunched back, hidden in the shadows, and waited, scarcely drawing a breath, his gaze fixed on the front door of his home with terrible intensity.

The door opened inward and for one brief moment the figure of Harry Wilsson was silhouetted against the hallway light behind him. Then he pressed the switch and the light went out, and he stepped out and closed the door solidly behind him.

Marvin Blake did not move as his friend and neighbor circled around the front of the convertible and got in the front seat.

The bedroom light remained on while Harry pressed the starter and his motor hummed into life and the convertible glided down the driveway in the starlight.

Watching him go, Marvin saw that he rolled downward

slowly without turning on his headlights to betray his leaving until he had turned into Lily Lane.

As though he had practiced that secretive method of departure often, Marvin thought with anguish.

And he could not help wondering how often he had.

The paramount feeling of which he was aware at that awful moment was one of unutterable sadness. He was numbed beyond any other emotion. There was an empty sickness in his stomach and he hugged his arms tightly about himself and trembled. Everything was over. Everything that had been good in life was now shattered.

He knew, with that sickness inside him, that he and Ellie could never pick up the pieces of their life again. No matter how hard they both tried. She was upstairs in their bedroom, lying in the bed that was still warm from their love-making.

He did not know what to do next. Now that Ellie was alone he could go in without, at least, causing a melodramatic scene. But it was too late in the night to pretend to Ellie that he had just walked up from the station after getting off the late train and had no idea he had been cuckolded during his absence. He looked at his watch and saw it was fifteen minutes after eleven. More than an hour since the train had stopped to let him off. He tried to think of some plausible story he could tell Ellie to explain the lapse of time, but even as he did so he knew it wasn't feasible.

With her sense of guilt, Ellie would never believe him. And, in truth, he didn't believe he'd be able to carry it off even if she allowed him to do so. In his heart he knew he *couldn't* go in and face Ellie now and pretend he knew nothing.

However, he could, perhaps, go in calmly and without anger, and explain to Ellie that he knew she had been closeted in the bedroom with Harry Wilsson, and listen to her tearful and shamefaced explanation of how it had happened. How Harry had just dropped in casually after dinner to keep her company during Marvin's last evening away from home, and how they'd had a few drinks together. And how the drinks had hit her unexpectedly and how it *happened*. Without her anticipating it. Without her wanting it. With her so tight she hadn't really known it *was* happening until it was all over. And how terribly ashamed she was and disgusted with herself, and how she still loved him dearly in spite of everything and if he could just find it in his heart to forgive her and to forget. . . .

He knew that was the way it would be if he went in now and told Ellie what he knew. And he didn't know whether he could stand that or not. Forgive Ellie?

He didn't know. When a man says he can forgive a person, exactly what does it mean? He can go through the outward motions. He can say the word out loud. But will he really mean the words he speaks aloud? Is true forgiveness honestly possible?

Certainly, he told himself, he could never forget. Never in all the world could he do that. Would it be possible to go on living together with the memory of this night always with him? He told himself firmly that he should try, for Sissy's sake. At least until the child was older and didn't need both parents so much. Then, if the situation proved to be unbearable, a quiet and unemotional separation could be arranged.

He had actually picked up his suitcase and started across the drive toward the front door when he stopped suddenly. He knew he could not do it. Not right then. Not while Ellie was still flushed from the caresses of her lover. He needed time to think things out and get a firm grip on himself. To evaluate what had happened, and to calmly plan the future.

He turned slowly and went down the winding driveway, carrying his suitcase with him. There was a southbound local due in a couple of hours that stopped at Sunray. No one need notice him get aboard it, and no one need know he had been in Sunray at all that night. He could go back to Miami, now that he knew the truth, and simply come back on the afternoon train as planned. By that time he would have things thought out clearly, and he would find a way, somehow, to go on and make a life with Ellie.

He felt awfully sorry for himself as he walked slowly and listlessly back down the driveway which he had walked up so blithely and happily only an hour before. He seemed to be standing off on the sidelines and looking at the pathetic figure of Marvin Blake wearily shuffling away from his home in the silence and loneliness of the night, and his heart bled for the man he watched.

Why had they done that to him? His wife and Harry Wilsson. How could they have done such a thing to a husband and a best friend? Didn't they care, or were they so thoughtless they hadn't realized what they were doing? Or so much in love that it didn't matter to them how they hurt Marvin Blake?

Ellie in love with Harry? No! Ellie was in love with him. She had been for ten whole years. You don't just change loves like you do a dress. A woman like Ellie doesn't.

And then he wondered if he knew what sort of person Ellie was after all. Did he really know her? Had he ever known her? Or was the Ellie in his mind just an image he had conjured up? What he wanted his wife to be, not necessarily what she was.

Certainly, the Ellie he thought he knew could not have fouled his bed tonight with another man.

Harry Wilsson, too. What did he actually know about him? The Harry that Marvin knew was laughing and gay and out-going. A congenial friend and drinking companion. The best man at his wedding, and the gravely understanding friend who had held his hand while Sissy was being born.

He had just reached the intersection of his driveway with Lily Lane when the whole thing really hit him for the first time. It hadn't been real up to that ponit. It was something he had realized and accepted, but with his mind only.

Not with his emotions. It hit him all at once and all over and terribly, and he pushed through the hibiscus hedge with his suitcase to the other side where he couldn't possibly be seen, and he dropped face downward onto the ground and began crying like a baby.

He didn't see how he was going to stand it. He didn't know what he was going to do.

4

By the time the local came through from Jacksonville, Marvin Blake knew what he was going to do. What he had to do.

Death was the only answer. Oblivion. He would be mourned for a time, but that would end and Marvin Blake would be forgotten.

Sissy would be all right. There was Marvin's insurance, his automobile agency, and a large equity in the house on Lily Lane. At the age of six, death did not impinge too harshly on a child's mind, and suicide would be practically a meaningless word to her.

While waiting for the train to reach Sunray Beach, Marvin planned everything carefully. It was most important, to avoid the slightest possibility of scandal involving

Sissy's mother, that no one should ever guess that Marvin Blake had come home this night.

There would be a police investigation, of course, and he realized they would discover that he had checked out of the Miami hotel that afternoon. There was even the possibility that they would discover the return half of his ticket had been used.

To meet that contingency he had decided to take the train back to Moonray Beach about thirty miles south, and get off there. He would get a room at the hotel, giving a fictitious Miami address, and while checking in he would mention something about having reached town on the earlier train from Miami.

In his room he would write a suicide note saying that he had started home that afternoon, but before reaching Sunray had realized he could not face his wife and daughter with the terrible weight of guilt he had on his conscience. He would intimate that he had been unfaithful to Ellie at the convention, and did not consider himself fit to go on living. And he would beg the forgiveness of Ellie and Sissy for what he was about to do.

He even knew exactly how he would commit the act. After writing the suicide note he would take off all his clothes and get in the bathtub and open the arteries in his wrists with a razor blade and let his life-blood ooze down the drain.

He was very careful to remain out of sight until the train came through. Sunray Beach had one night policeman who casually patrolled the streets at night in his police car, but he was just about the only local resident awake after midnight, and Marvin did not even see his car making the rounds while he skulked at the far end of the deserted parking lot at the depot, and he watched the dimly lighted station nervously as train-time neared, hoping that no one else had decided to catch the early morning train into Miami.

No car had driven up to the station and there was no sign of life there when he heard the oncoming train whistle loudly in the distance, a mournful, eerie sound in the night silence which sounded to him like a dirge for Marvin Blake who was soon to die.

He remained hidden in the shadow of a palm tree while the short train wheezed in, and was relieved when the single day coach stopped almost directly in front of him.

A trainman stepped down swinging an electric lantern, and Marvin stepped forward with his suitcase and climbed aboard without looking at the man.

The rear seat of the coach was vacant and he dropped into it with his suitcase beside him and leaned back with his hat tipped down over his face and with a dollar bill ready in his right hand.

The train pulled out toward Miami smoothly almost before he was comfortably settled, and he waited a long time, watching beneath the brim of his hat until he saw the conductor's feet pause in the aisle beside him.

He extended the bill toward him and muttered sleepily, "One way to Moonray Beach, please."

The bill was whisked from his grasp, and he kept his hand extended, palm upward, until the conductor dropped his change and receipt into it and moved away.

He waited until the train came to a full stop before getting up from the seat and stepping off the train. Moonray Beach was almost twice as large as Sunray, and there were half a dozen people standing around the station, but none of them so much as glanced at Marvin as he carried his suitcase briskly to Main Street.

He had vaguely hoped to find a bar open where he could stop for a few drinks before going on to the hotel, but in this he was disappointed. Everything was closed, and he trudged the block and a half to a dingy hotel which had known better times and was putting up a listless struggle against the competition of modern motels which had sprung up on the outskirts.

The small lobby was ill-lighted and empty except for an old man dozing behind the registration desk with a streak of tobacco juice running down his chin from the corner of his mouth.

He blinked rheumy eyes open and stood up slowly when Marvin rapped on the desk in front of him, and he yawned widely and reckoned he did have a vacant room when Marvin asked for one.

He signed a registration card, "Marvin Blake," and added the name of the Miami hotel at which he had been staying. As he pushed the card back he said carelessly, "I came in on the ten o'clock train, but didn't know I was going to be stuck for the night," and the clerk nodded without interest and slid a key numbered 201 across to him and mumbled, "Right up at the head of them stairs."

Marvin took the key and started to turn away, then hesitated and said, "I need a night-cap real bad." He got a ten-dollar bill from his wallet and spread it on the counter. "That's yours if you can scare up a bottle I can take to my room."

The old man looked down at the bill avidly and said, "No place open in town this time uh night. Tell yuh what though, Mister. If you don't mind a couple of drinks off the top of a bottle of Four Roses, I reckon I might fix you up."

Marvin told him he didn't mind at all, and the clerk went around behind the switchboard and came back with an opened fifth. The couple of drinks that were missing had been healthy slugs, but there was still more than enough left in the bottle to get Marvin drunker than he had ever been in his life, so he took it and shoved the bill over and picked up his suitcase in the other hand and went up the stairs to his room.

Inside, the room was fairly clean and as impersonal as every hotel room. Marvin set his suitcase down at the foot of the bed and took off his hat and coat, then carried the bottle of whiskey into the bathroom. He found two water-glasses there, and uncorked the bottle and poured one of them half-full. He was surprised to see how his hand shook as he did so, and he realized that he really did need that bottle.

He filled the glass to the brim from the tap, and stood there and forced the entire glassful down his throat without taking it away from his lips.

It hit the pit of his stomach like fire, and slowly spread through the rest of his body.

He poured the glass almost half-full a second time and

added water, and carried bottle and glass back and set them on top of the bureau.

Then he unfastened his suitcase and opened it, and got out a pad of yellow, ruled paper and a fresh packet of razor blades.

He sat on the edge of the bed with the blades lying beside him and the pad on his knees, and got out his pen and wrote as firmly as he could: "To whom it may concern."

He paused, staring down at the words, trying to get them into focus, angry because his hand was still so unsteady. He decided he needed another drink before he could get on with the job.

He went to the bureau and slowly emptied the glass again, shuddering convulsively as he did so, then sat on the edge of the bed again and laboriously began composing his death message.

5

Timothy Rourke, star reporter for the Miami *News*, awoke that next morning languidly and slowly, with an almost unbelievable sense of physical well-being flooding through him as he became pleasantly aware of bright sunshine and fresh sea air flooding through the open window beside his bed, and listened to the unexcited twittering of birds in a tree just outside.

He had no semblance of a hangover, no taste of dry asbestos in his mouth. He had no idea what time it was and, very happily, he did not care to know. He blinked up drowsily at the low ceiling of the motel room and consciously willed himself to drift into a self-congratulatory reverie that was half-sleeping and half-waking.

This, by God, was what happened to a man when he went to bed stone, cold sober, all by himself in his own monastic bed, and slept the entire night through without a single nightmare, without once waking to the taste of sour retching in his throat.

He ought to do this sort of thing oftener, he told himself sternly; and he wondered sleepily why he didn't, and he vaguely pitied himself because he knew very well why he didn't do it more often.

It was because he just didn't have the requisite will-power. Last night, for instance, had required no will-power at all. It was purely accidental and not of his own volition that he had turned in at eleven o'clock without a drink in his belly except the two cocktails he had allowed himself at dinner in Jacksonville. He had held himself down to those two at dinner because he wanted to cover another hundred miles or so toward Miami before stopping to spend the night, and he *did* have enough common sense and will-power to keep himself fairly sober while driving on the highway, and it had given him something to look forward to as he drove southward through the night.

So it was that when he pulled off the road and turned in at the Sunray Beach Motel a little after ten o'clock it had been with the happy anticipation of belting down half a dozen or more fast slugs before turning in for the night. But he made the mistake of signing the register and paying for his room before casually asking the motel clerk where he would have to go to find a drink.

The clerk had appeared slyly pleased to inform him that Sunray's only bar closed promptly at ten o'clock and the nearest place open at that hour was thirty-three miles down the road.

And, Nossir, said the clerk, he sure didn't have a bottle around the place. He didn't have a license to sell liquor, and he never touched the stuff his own self.

Timothy Rourke lay in bed and grinned now as he recalled how angry and outraged he had been at that sorry state of affairs last night. He had killed his own travelling bottle in Atlanta the previous evening, and had stupidly neglected to buy another during the day. He had been sorely tempted to drive on thirty-three miles, but a small streak of self-respect had refused to allow him to give the clerk the satisfaction of demanding his money back so he could go on to where a drink would be available.

He wasn't a dipso, damn it. He had always said he could take the stuff or leave it alone. Who the hell *had* to have a drink? So he had stalked out of the office and driven around in front of the empty unit and gone to bed. And to instant, dreamless sleep.

And now he felt blissfully pleased with himself and deliciously hungry, and he lay in bed another five minutes savoring the pleasant sensation and wondering why he didn't try it more often.

His watch on the bedside table said it was nine-thirty when he finally threw off the light cover and slid out of bed. He showered swiftly, and shaved, and as he dressed he planned what he would have for breakfast. By God, he was hungry. And not even slightly thirsty. He righteously told himself he didn't give a whoop in hell *when* Sunray's only bar opened for business in the morning. What he wanted was food, in huge quantities.

He had noticed a coffee shop next to the motel office last night, and he strode out impatiently into the bright sunlight and crossed the parking area toward it. This morning there were only three cars besides his own in the rectangle although it had been almost full when he turned in last night.

The coffee shop was bright and clean and cheerful, with a long lunch counter and a row of unoccupied stools in front of it. There were tables along the wall, and a young couple with two small children sat at one of them in the corner.

Rourke went blithely to the counter and sat down, and the waitress opened a dog-eared breakfast menu in front of him. She was big-busted and big-butted, and had a pleasantly bovine face, and she asked cheerfully, "What's it going to be this morning?"

"Food," the reporter told her with gusto. He pushed the printed menu away and said, "Toast. With lots of butter spread on while it's hot. Do you have any sausage?"

She nodded. "Country-style patties. It's home-made and real tasty."

"Just what the doctor ordered," he told her happily. "Three patties of tasty sausage, well done and very crisp. And three scrambled eggs. Do you think you could use your influence with the cook," he added earnestly, "to get the eggs scrambled lightly . . . so they're real fluffy? He spread out his hands appealingly and smiled, and she smiled back and said, "You just bet I will. If there's anything makes me sick to my stomach in the morning it's old, tired, tough scrambled eggs." She started to turn away and asked over her shoulder, "Hash-brown potatoes with that?"

"Lord, yes," he told her enthusiastically. "Hash-browns, certainly. And a cup of coffee to start, if you don't mind."

My God, he thought as he watched the wriggling of her wide buttocks as she went back to give his order, how long had it been since he could even face the thought of fried potatoes for breakfast. Now his mouth actually watered at the prospect.

She returned with a large china mug of fresh, very hot and very strong coffee and placed it in front of him, and took a step backward from the counter and folded her arms across her ample bosom and said, "Isn't it just awful about last night?"

Rourke took an appreciative sip of the good coffee and wondered why they didn't make it like that in Miami any more. "What," he asked, looking across the rim of the steaming cup at her, "is awful about last night?"

"Didn't you hear about it?" she asked eagerly, planting both hands on her hips and leaning forward. "It's been on the radio since seven o'clock."

"What's been on the radio?"

"Murder. That's what. Right here in Sunray. Can you beat it? Lordy, it sends the shivers up and down my spine every time I think of it."

"It happens," said Rourke sententiously, "in the best of communities."

"I guess so, but you just never think . . . you know? Like that book somebody wrote: 'It can't happen here'. But it *did* happen here. Right last night. While everybody was sound asleep."

Timothy Rourke tilted the thick mug in both hands and drank as deeply as he dared of the hot liquid.

"Everybody in town wasn't asleep," he argued gently. "There was the murderer and the murderee. Who were they?"

"Mrs. Blake. That's who. One of the nicest, sweetest women you'd ever know. You're a stranger in town, aren't you?" She half-closed her eyes to study his thin and deeply-lined face. "Just stopping through?"

Rourke nodded. "On my way to Miami. Tell me more about your murder. I'm a newspaper reporter."

"Are you, now? From Miami? I guess it'll make the headlines, all right. Put Sunray right on the map. Maybe you'll write it up for your paper, huh?"

"Maybe. If so, I'll want to quote you, of course. In an exclusive interview this morning, this reporter was told by . . . what is your name?"

"Me? Mabel Handel. But you wouldn't put my name in, would you? I don't know anything except what I've heard."

"You're my exclusive source of information," he assured her solemnly. "Except you haven't told me very much yet. A woman named Mrs. Blake was murdered in Sunray last night. When? Where? How? By whom? Why?"

"Well, I . . . sometime in the night. I guess they don't know just when. Sissy found her this morning. Imagine that? Isn't it just horrible? Sissy's the Blakes' little girl. Six years old, I guess. She's a darling little girl. Think of it! Her own mother murdered in the bedroom right next to hers in the night, and she never knew. Not until this morning. Not until she got up and peeked in her momma's room and saw her lying there. Stiff and cold and strangled. Naked, they say. Naked as a jaybird in her own bed. Can you *imagine?*"

Rourke said, "You're doing all right, Mabel. That's the when, where, and how. Now: by whom, and why?"

"Nobody knows who did it. Must have been a tramp, they think. A sex maniac, I say. Ellie Blake was a mighty pretty woman. Young enough to . . . you know? Not more than thirty, I guess. Why else would anybody do it? In bed like that . . . and naked. You can't tell me it wasn't a sex crime."

"Where was her husband at the time?"

"That's just it. At an automobile dealers' convention in Miami. He's got the Ford agency here. One of our prominent citizens. He's real nice, Marv is. Stops in here for coffee sometimes. Always got a comeback when you kid him. Not smart-alecky or fresh, you know. He and Ellie were the sweetest couple. Neither one of them ever looked at anyone else. And is he crazy about his Sissy? That's the little girl, you know. Poor Marvin! I don't know *how* he'll face this. Just think of it!"

The ping of a bell from the kitchen drew her attention, and she returned with a tray loaded down with more breakfast than Timothy Rourke had looked in the face for many years.

The toast was a beautiful golden brown and each slice was inundated with fresh country butter. The sausage patties were darkly crisp on the outside and tenderly tangy underneath; the eggs were, indeed, gently and lovingly scrambled to a creamy and fluffy deliciousness, and the hashed-brown potatoes were definitely a culinary triumph.

After setting the dishes out in front of him, Mabel had to go to the cash register to ring up the bill for the young couple and their two children who were leaving, and Rourke had an opportunity to sample each item and miraculously discover that his appetite was unimpaired before Mabel returned and stood before him again and asked, "You going to write up a story about it, for your paper in Miami?"

Rourke chewed fast and swallowed deeply and gulped some hot coffee. He said firmly, "Anything that will give me the slightest excuse to linger in Sunray for another night and expose me to food like this tomorrow morning will be a gift from the Gods. Certainly, I think the Miami *News* needs a special correspondent to handle the Blake murder case, and I just happen to be it." He demolished another slice of toast and forked more scrambled egg into his mouth and chewed vigorously. "Where do I find your local police department?"

"Right down the highway four blocks and turn to your left on Main Street. It's right on your left . . . the City Hall and all. Gee, it's exciting, isn't it? Will my name really be in the paper?"

"Mabel Handel," Rourke assured her, "will be prominently featured as this reporter's most reliable source of information. Now then. How about some more background on the Blakes? Marvin and Ellie? And you call the little daughter Sissy? Did you say she's six?"

"Everybody calls her Sissy," Mabel told him vaguely. "I suppose she has another name, but *I* never heard it. Ellie and Marvin . . . they were sweethearts in high school, and got married a couple of years after he graduated and went to work in Mr. Harper's garage. That was Ellie's papa. But it wasn't like he married the boss's daughter trying to get ahead in the world," she hurried on. "Right after they got married, Marvin leased a shop of his own, and then got the Ford Agency. He's done real well, I guess. Everyone likes him . . . and Ellie, too. They're about as much as what you might call society as Sunray Beach has, I guess. Were, I should say. My goodness, I just can't get it through my head that Ellie is actually dead. When I think of poor little Sissy without any mama any more, it just about breaks my heart." Big tears welled out of her eyes and streamed down her cheeks. She sniffled loudly and put her apron up to her face and turned her back on Rourke with heaving shoulders.

He continued munching on his food, but it tasted not quite as good as it had in the beginning. Mabel returned in a moment, her eyes red-rimmed, to refill his coffee cup, and he pushed the half-emptied plates away from him with a sigh. "I haven't eaten as much of anything as good for years, Mabel. Tell your cook so, will you?"

"I sure will." She smiled at him diffidently. "You never did tell me your name."

"Rourke. Tim Rourke."

"You staying here at the motel?"

"As long as I'm in town. Depends on what I find out down at the police station. In the meantime, you keep your ears open for any news, huh? I'll be back."

"I sure will, Mr. Rourke."

"Tim . . . if you're going to be Mabel," he told her with a grin as he slid off his stool.

"Sure . . . Tim." She walked down behind the counter to the cash register, totalling up his bill on her pad with a worried frown, and she handed it to him hesitantly, saying, "Prices sure are sky-high, but I got to charge what the boss says."

Rourke grinned cheerfully when he saw that her total was less than a dollar and a half. He put two ones on top of it and told her, "The expense account will go that far, Mabel." He turned toward the door and paused to ask with assumed disinterest, "There is a bar in town, isn't there?"

"Right on Main Street just past City Hall. But it won't be opened until twelve o'clock."

"Naturally not," said Rourke, trying to repress his bitterness. "And I bet it closes at ten o'clock at night, too."

"It sure does. They say Sunray's pretty much a ten o'clock town." She laughed lightly. "How'd you guess?"

Rourke said, "It just *feels* like that sort of town, Mabel," and went out the front door with a wave of his hand.

6

Chief of Police Ollie Jenson was a harassed and unhappy man. He had a stomach ulcer which he had lived with for going-on twenty years, and which he had learned to keep under pretty fair control by nipping gently throughout the day on a bottle of Indian River moonshine which he kept concealed in the bottom right-hand drawer of his desk at police headquarters. By trial and error he had determined many years ago that legal, bonded whiskey was no good for that medicinal purpose. He had his own private theory that the coloring matter added after distillation was an irritant that caused a man's ulcer to act up. Besides, the moonshine cost him nothing; a prerogative of his official position.

Chief Jenson also had a sharp-tongued and nagging wife whom he had lived with for slightly more than twenty years. He couldn't keep her under control by nipping at moonshine at home because she was rabidly Temperance and there hadn't been a drink in their house since that memorable day nineteen years ago when she had mistakenly poured a cup of colorless fluid out of a Mason jar standing in plain sight on one of her kitchen shelves (the purloined letter technique) into a pot of shredded cabbage, thinking it was vinegar. The local pastor and his wife were guests at dinner that night, and the shredded cabbage did not get eaten. Neither did Ollie Jenson ever bring another innocent-looking Mason jar home with him.

Ollie also had a sprightly, teen-aged daughter named Mary Lou. She was not overly bright, but Nature had compensated for that lack by endowing her with a pair of superb physical appurtenances which had been widely admired and discussed by the male youth of Sunray since Mary Lou reached her fifteenth year. While vaguely aware of this situation, Chief Jenson had not been unduly worried by it until the past few months when Mary Lou had begun staying out too late and too often with the son of the local banker who owned a hot-rod flivver. Ollie was not an overly suspicious father, and he had an indulgent idea that kids would be kids no matter what a parent said or did about it, but he suspected (privately and unhappily) that neither his daughter nor the banker's son had a thorough grounding in the theory and use of contraceptives, and he saw no way to provide them with such knowledge.

It was not a matter he could discuss with his wife.

On top of those harassments of more-or-less long-standing, this morning now, there was this murder dumped in his lap. It was the first murder that had ever occurred in

Sunray Beach, and it was a real nasty kind of thing.

That nice Ellie Blake. Strangled in her own bed in the middle of the night, and not one single clue to the perpetrator of the foul deed that you could lay your hands on. It had to be some stranger, of course. Some hitchhiker or bum passing through town. It couldn't be a local resident. Why, Ollie reckoned Ellie Blake was just about the most-respected and best-liked woman in town. And old Marv!

Everybody liked Marvin Blake. He didn't have an enemy in the world. Look at the way he ran his garage and automobile agency. Always gave a man a fair deal for his money, and leaned over backward to give a little bit more on a trade-in than the book allowed. Good, upright, church-going people, with money in the bank and a decent mortgage on a nice house that was getting paid off regular every year.

And that cute little girl of theirs. Apple of her daddy's eye, Sissy was. Bright as they come, and pretty as a picture. And Ellie had been noted as a mighty fine mother, too. Keeping up with the latest stuff on child psychology, but with a goodly leavening of old-fashioned motherly love to keep things in balance and make Sissy into a normal, happy child.

Thinking about Sissy and that terrible scene in the upstairs bedroom of the Blake house early that morning, Chief Jenson sighed deeply and looked at his watch. Almost ten o'clock.

Most days he carefully waited until ten o'clock for his first nip of ulcer remedy, but this day was different. He shifted his solid bulk in the swivel chair behind his desk and leaned forward with a slight grunt to open the bottom right-hand drawer. He withdrew a flat, unmarked quart bottle that was a little more than half-full of shine, and worried the cork out with his teeth. Tomorrow morning was one of Jed's three-a-week delivery days. He put the bottle to his mouth and swallowed two long, smooth gulps just as a brisk knock sounded on the door of his office.

He lowered the bottle deliberately and replaced the cork, deposited it carefully in the drawer and pushed the door shut with his foot. He wiped his mouth unhurriedly with the back of his hand, and only then did he lean forward to touch a button on the underside of his desk which electrically unlocked the outer door.

This gadget was practically the only bit of modern equipment belonging to the Sunray Beach police department and was one of Chief Jenson's most prized possessions. He had seen it advertised at $9.98 in a mail order catalog ten years ago and had promptly ordered it and had it installed on his door to prevent anyone from walking in unannounced while the chief might be taking a nip of his ulcer remedy.

It was an ingenious device which caused the door to latch automatically each time it was closed, and to stay locked until Ollie pressed the button beneath his desk which activated the lock. Prior to its installation, the chief had had the choice of either leaving his door unlocked and risking the unannounced entrance of any one of the friendly citizens of Sunray at an embarrassing moment, or keeping the door locked at all times and being forced to get up from his desk and waddle around to unlatch it each time he had a visitor. Now, he could take his time about pressing the button, secure in the knowledge that no one could enter, yet be ready to greet them comfortably in his chair behind the desk, giving the impression that the door must have stuck, somehow, and that Ollie had no idea how it happened to come unstuck when it did.

All three members of his Force knew about the automatic locking device, of course, and waited patiently after knocking until they heard the click of the release catch. Other visitors were wont to twist and rattle the knob, and sometimes shout loudly to attract the chief's attention, and thus he was able to foretell rather accurately whether one of his own men or some outsider would come through the door after he unlocked it.

This morning it was Ralph Harris who pushed the door open and stepped inside. He was nominally on night duty (from 12 to 8) but with the Blake murder and all, Chief Jenson had issued orders that morning requiring the entire Force to remain on duty throughout the day. Harris had been assigned to remain at Headquarters to answer telephone calls and coordinate the search for the murderer; young Leroy Smith, technological expert, was currently on duty at the Blake house with his fingerprint kit and special vacuum cleaner gathering clues and collecting evidence; and Randy Perkins, grizzled veteran of the Force, was out driving Sunray's only Police Cruiser up and down the highways and byways surrounding the town looking for some unknown transient who would be unable to provide an alibi for the preceding night and could be pulled in and charged with the crime.

Officer Harris closed the door behind him and reported, "There's a newspaper reporter from Miami wants to see you, Chief. Name of Rourke. From the Miami *News*. I told him I'd see."

"Miami *News*?" said Chief Ollie Jenson with a frown. "You know we don't want no publicity, Ralph. Daytona and Jacksonville papers both telephoned up and I told 'em we had no comment." He paused, blinking his eyelids fretfully and glancing over at an open copy of yesterday's Miami *News* which lay on the desk. "Rourke, you say? Would that be Timothy Rourke?" He put his finger on a front-page by-lined story. "Big-shot city reporter, huh? This here's an interview he had with the mayor of Miami."

"I guess his name's Timothy Rourke. You want to talk to him?"

Chief Jenson sighed unhappily. "Send him in. I guess there ain't nothing new we got on the Blake case, is there?"

"Nothing I heard." Harris backed out of the door and it clicked shut behind him. Ollie waited with his finger touching the release button, and pressed it when footsteps came down the hall and stopped outside. The knob turned and Timothy Rourke walked in briskly.

The chief pushed back his swivel chair and half stood, leaning forward with his left hand on the desk and his right extended toward his visitor. "Glad to meetcha, Mister Rourke. The Miami *News* is right on the job, huh?"

"I happened to be passing through and heard about your murder," Rourke told him honestly, sniffing with pleasure as he shook the chief's hand and caught the faint but unmistakable odor of sour-mash on his breath. He pulled a chair closer to the desk and relaxed in it, crossing one bony leg over the other. "What are the actual facts?"

"There just ain't much to go on, Mr. Rourke. I got the

call a little after six this morning. Minerva Wilsson phoned me. That's Harry Wilsson's wife. They're the Blakes' closest friends in town. The little girl had phoned Minerva ... that's Sissy, you know ... soon's she woke up and stuck her head into her mamma's bedroom and seen her lying there in bed like that. She knew the Wilsson's phone number and it was natural she'd call Minerva. She went right over and took one look and called me.

"Strangled to death in her bed, she was. Ellie. Mrs. Blake. Cold and already getting pretty stiff. Doc Higgens made a guess it happened around midnight. And that, by God and by Henry, is just about all, Mr. Rourke. Some damn hobo is my guess. Burglar, maybe. Doors were all locked, but there's a front window in the living room unlatched and up an inch or two. Gravel path underneath it that won't take tracks."

"Any sign of a struggle in the bedroom?"

"Not so's you'd notice. She was undressed and the bedcovers thrown back. Not even a nightgown, but ... it was a warm night. Her clothes was kinda tossed on the floor by the bed."

"Had she been sexually attacked?"

Chief Jenson blinked at him. "Raped, you mean?"

Rourke shrugged. "Maybe molested is a better word?"

"I don't know how you'd go about telling ... a married woman and all." Ollie paused awkwardly. "No blood or like that."

"There are medical tests," Rourke told him. "An examination for seminal fluid in the vaginal passage."

"Well, yeh, sure," Ollie agreed uncomfortably. "Doc Higgens is making the autopsy. He'll find out for sure I reckon. If it was that, you can bet that's why she was murdered. Man couldn't do nothing like that to Ellie with*out* he strangled her first, I'll give you that. Mighty fine woman."

"Anything missing from the house? Any signs of burglary?"

"That's hard to say. Maybe Marvin can help us there when he gets back from Miami this afternoon. Going to be an almighty shock to him, I can tell you." Jenson shook his head dolefully. "Plumb crazy about Ellie, he was. And her about him, too. Not a nicer couple in this whole town than Marvin and Ellie Blake."

"What are you doing about finding the murderer?"

"Everything I know to do, I can tell you that. There's word out that anybody seen a suspicious stranger hanging around yesterday is to report on it. I got the State Police alerted to watch out for hitch-hikers. My best man's over to the house now, fingerprinting and working one of those special vacuum cleaners for any clues he can find. I got another man covering all the roads in and out of Sunray.

"It seems a little late for that now," murmured Rourke.

"What else is there to do?" Chief Jenson spread out his hands and glared at the reporter from Miami. "Maybe we ain't no big city police force, but you tell me what else the Miami police would be doing. First murder we ever had in Sunray Beach, I can tell you that. Mighty nice, quiet, friendly little town. We'll get him, don't you worry. Not so many strangers around this time of year that somebody won't've noticed him. I figure he must have hung around some and cased the house, you see. Maybe saw Ellie go in and out and got ideas about her. You know. She had a figure a man *would* get ideas about."

"The kind that wanted men to notice her?"

"Now don't be getting no wrong ideas." Chief Jenson frowned portentiously. "Maybe she did shake it a little bit, but that was just her way. A man didn't know her, he might get the idea she'd be an easy lay, but he'd be Godalmighty wrong. And it's my theory that's maybe what did happen last night. He must of waited till after she and Sissy went to bed and then sneaked in and upstairs thinking she'd, well . . . welcome him, like, to bed. And then he had to shut her up from screaming, and . . . and . . . ." The chief paused and dragged a handkerchief out from his hip pocket and mopped his perspiring face.

"How would a stranger in town have known she and her child were alone in the house last night?"

"He could of asked around easy, I guess. Everybody knew Marv was in Miami at that car dealers' convention and wasn't due home until today. House is off by itself pretty much."

"Has the husband been notified?" asked Rourke briskly.

"I didn't see any need to. I always say, bad news travels fast enough without any help. What could Marvin do about it? Let the poor devil finish up his convention and be happy while he can. Time enough for him to find out when he gets back on the train."

Timothy Rourke shrugged and looked at his watch. "Do you know what train he's due in on?"

"Three-thirty this afternoon. It doesn't leave Miami till noon. Last night was the big night of the convention for the boys to make whoopee, and they'll all be nursing king-sized hangovers, I reckon. Including Marv. Not that he's a drinking man, you understand," Ollie went on hastily. "But being away from home to a convention with the rest of the boys and all . . . you know?"

Rourke nodded absently and muttered, "I should call in a story, and I could use a quote from the bereaved husband. Do you know the hotel Blake is staying at?"

"Convention headquarters was the Atlantic Palms. I know that much."

"Use your telephone?" Rourke reached out a long arm for it and lifted the receiver.

"You going to try and call Marv from here? That'll be long distance and mighty expensive. There's a pay phone . . . ."

"Long distance please," Rourke interrupted him, speaking into the mouthpiece. "Charge it," he muttered to the agitated chief of police, and into the phone he said, "A person to person call to Miami charged to credit card number . . . ." He paused and screwed up his face and repeated a series of digits from memory.

"That's right," he told the operator. "I want to speak to Mr. Marvin Blake at the Atlantic Palms Hotel in Miami. I don't know the phone number. Yes, I'll hold on."

While he waited, Chief Jenson sank back in his creaking swivel chair and regarded him wonderingly, "I sure envy you your job, Mister, but I'm just as glad you're doing it instead of me this afternoon. I been racking my brains how in hell you break it to a man that his wife's been murdered while he was out having fun at a convention, and I . . . ." He broke off as Rourke spoke into the telephone, "What's that, operator? Are you certain? Let me speak to the desk clerk at the Atlantic Palms instead of Mr. Blake."

He put his hand over the receiver and frowned across the desk at Jenson. "They say that Marvin Blake checked out of the hotel yesterday afternoon."

"Can't be. I know the convention lasted through last night. It was the big banquet and shindig. Stands to reason . . . ."

"Hello." Rourke spoke into the telephone again. "This is a reporter from the *News* calling long distance from Sunray Beach. It's extremely important that I contact Mr. Marvin Blake before he catches the noon train from Miami. He was at an automobile dealer's convention which didn't end until this morning."

He paused and listened thoughtfully to a scratchy voice coming over the wire from Miami. After a time, he said, "I see. Well, thank you very much." He hung up shaking his head.

"That seems to be definite. Blake checked out of the Atlantic Palms a little before four o'clock yesterday afternoon even though the convention did run through last night and most of the delegates are still there right now."

Chief Ollie Jenson's jaw hung open slackly. "Yesterday afternoon? I don't get it. Where'd Marv go? He's not due home until today. He wouldn't just walk out on the convention. It don't stand to reason."

Timothy Rourke's eyes were feverishly bright and he reached a thin hand for the phone again. "I think we'd better try to find out where Marvin Blake was while his wife was getting herself murdered. Operator? Another person to person call to Miami charged to the same card number. You got it? Michael Shayne." He gave her the redheaded detective's office number and Chief Jenson leaned forward nervously.

"Hey. Mike Shayne! That's that private detective in Miami ain't it? I don't know as I like you calling him. . . ."

"Hi, Mike," Rourke said into the phone. "Tim Rourke. I'm calling from Sunray Beach where we had a sex murder last night. Doing anything the next half hour?"

From Miami, Michael Shayne said, "Not a thing, Tim."

"Write this down. Marvin Blake from Sunray Beach. Delegate to the auto dealers' convention at Atlantic Palms Hotel which ended last night. His wife was murdered here at midnight. Blake has been expected home on the noon train from Miami, but I just talked to the hotel and they tell me he checked out at four yesterday. If you get over there right away you may find some of the delegates who know him. Get anything you can on his whereabouts last night . . . why he checked out. You can call me at . . . no, wait a minute. I'll be moving around up here. I'll call you in an hour. Got all that?"

Shayne said, "I'm on my way."

Timothy Rourke hung up and stared moodily across the desk at Sunray's chief of police. "You say you've got a man on the Blake house?"

"Leroy Smith. He's a real smart young . . . ."

"How do I get to the Blake house?" Rourke was on his feet and turned toward the door.

"Wait a minute now. I ain't one bit sure I want any newspaper reporters messing around . . . ."

"Nuts," said Rourke dispassionately. "You've got one whether you like it or not." He went out the door while Jenson was laboriously pushing himself upright.

7

Leroy Smith was a sober, serious and sincere young man of twenty-two with a crew-cut, and he wore his neatly-pressed khaki uniform of the Sunray Beach Police Department with prideful self-consciousness. Since the age of twelve, his one desire and ambition in life had been to become a member of the F.B.I., and he felt that his appointment by Chief Jenson as a probationary patrolman last year was the first major step toward achieving his ambition.

One decent break was all he needed. One major case which he could solve triumphantly and single-handedly by application of the rules of Scientific Crime Investigation as set forth in his books on the subject might well bring him nation-wide prominence and a personal invitation from J. Edgar Hoover to appear in Washington forthwith.

After eight months of patient waiting, Leroy Smith's big

chance had finally come to him. Here he was, in charge of
a big important murder case. Well, practically in charge.
There was no doubt in his own mind that the solution of
the crime was strictly up to him.

Hadn't Chief Jenson said so this morning when he dis-
patched him to the Blake house to conduct a thorough and
Scientific Investigation at the Scene of the Crime?

"I reckon it's up to you, Leroy. Fingerprints and all like
that. Mighty glad I got a smart young man like you to take
charge else I'd have to call in the State Police and have them
traipsing all over and stealing the credit. Might be some
footprints under that big front window you could get one
of them there things of. I reckon that's where he got into
the house, all the other ground-floor doors and windows
being locked."

"A moulage, Chief," Smith had supplied eagerly. "Sure,
I've got the material for taking impressions. I'll stop by
Mom's to borrow a double boiler for heating it. And I'll
get her vacuum cleaner to help gather up clues. Might be
stuff on the floor inside the window fell out of his cuffs
when he crawled in. Distinctive grains of sand that'll show
a special region he came from, cigarette ashes that can be
analyzed."

"Sure," said Ollie Jenson vaguely. "You go right to it,
Leroy. We'll pick the son-of-a-bitch up, don't you worry,
and might be your evidence will clinch the case against
him."

Unfortunately, the entire area beneath the front window
had a thick layer of gravel over a hard surface that couldn't
possibly take a footprint, and a careful dusting of the in-

terior and exterior of window and sill with his specially prepared fingerprint powders and an ostrich feather duster
brought no discernible fingerprints to light. Neither did the
living room floor inside the window provide anything that
looked faintly like a clue although he went over it carefully
with his mother's vacuum sweeper equipped with a special
filter attachment of methacrylate plastic using a 22-cm
Whatman No. 1 filter which he had ordered personally
from a specialty company in Berkeley, California, when he
first joined the Force and had kept in readiness ever since
for just such an emergency as this.

There was one possible clue in the otherwise immaculate
living room which Leroy observed, although he was inclined to discount the importance of it. This was the
presence of two highball glasses sitting side by side on the
low coffee table in front of the settee against the right-hand
wall. Both glasses held a small residue of faintly amber-
colored liquid which Leroy intended to test for alcoholic
contents later on in his own laboratory at home, and he had
carefully dusted both glasses for fingerprints and lifted
several clean ones with scotch tape from each glass which
were clearly from two different persons when examined
under a magnifying glass. Those taken from one glass were
clearly identifiable as the victim's by comparison with other
prints of Ellie's which Leroy had lifted from articles on her
dressing table and in the kitchen, while those from the
second glass were surely from some person who had sat in
the living room with her the previous night having a friendly
nightcap.

The reason Leroy didn't have too much hope that

eventual identification of the second set of prints would lead to the criminal was his disinclination to believe that Mrs. Blake could possibly have sat down in the living room to have a drink with the man who was later to strangle her upstairs in her own bed.

Ellie Blake had been a real nice, quiet, home-loving wife and mother, who might take a social drink now and then with a friend who dropped in after supper, but she certainly wasn't the type to have a drink with a strange hitch-hiker who had murder on his mind.

As soon as news of her death spread through town, Leroy was positive in his own mind that whoever had that night-cap with her prior to her murder would come forward and report it to the police, and it was probably silly to save the fingerprints on the glass, but he had them carefully preserved nonetheless.

Other than those two highball glasses sitting companionably side by side in the living room Leroy Smith had not discovered a single clue of seeming significance in the entire empty and silent house of death.

There were only two doors leading into the house. The rear door into the kitchen was securely bolted on the inside. The front door, which automatically locked when it was pulled shut and required a Yale key to unlock it, showed no sign of having been forced. Dusting for fingerprints on both inside and outside knobs (going on the theory that the murderer might have simply walked out the front door and pulled it shut behind him) had brought negative results. There were fragmentary prints and blurs on both knobs, but nothing conclusive.

So far as Leroy Smith could ascertain, there was nothing out of place, nothing to indicate that murder had been committed, although he had examined the entire premises minutely and in accord with all the rules on Examination Of The Scene Of The Crime as set forth by the criminological experts who had authored all the volumes in his private library.

The kitchen was neat and shining and spic-and-span, just as any good housewife would leave it after the evening meal was done and the child had been bedded down for the night. The dining-room was immaculate, and there were only those two empty glasses in the living room to give their mute evidence of an after-supper visitor.

Upstairs, there were two bedrooms and a large bathroom between them, with a door entering into it from each bedroom. At the head of the stairs, which led up from the entrance hallway leading between kitchen and living room, you turned to the right to enter the master bedroom that had been occupied by Marvin and Ellie Blake. Directly on the left from the stair landing was a door leading into the only bathroom which was bolted on the inside. As previously noted, the bathroom could also be entered by doors from either the master bedroom or Sissy's room, which was beyond the bathroom from the head of the stairs.

So far as Leroy Smith had been able to discover, there were no significant indications or clues in the upper part of the house. To be perfectly honest, he had only opened the door of Sissy's room and glanced inside hastily before closing it. What could even a Scientific Crime Investigator hope to discover in the bedroom of a six-year-old who had tenderly been tucked into bed the preceding night by her loving mother and slept until early morning when Sissy had wakened a little before six o'clock (according to her own story babbled tearfully to Aunt Minerva Wilsson) and gone through the bathroom to open the door into the master bedroom to discover the twisted, nude, cold, dead body of her beloved mamma stretched out on top of the double bed without a stitch of clothing or bedcovers on her?

Horrified, and not at all really understanding why her "Mommy" did not respond to her, the little girl had run out into the hallway and down the stairs into the living room where she had dialled the Wilsson telephone number because it was the one most familiar to her. "Aunt Minerva" and "Uncle Harry" were the two adult persons in Sunray whom she knew best and trusted most, and felt the closest to in the entire town.

No. One couldn't expect to find any clues in Sissy's bedroom. Leroy had contented himself with swiftly glancing inside, wincing and gritting his teeth as he let his imagination take hold and he visualized the little girl awaking that morning happily with the early morning sunlight streaming in the window, thinking to herself that this was the day her Daddy would be coming back from the convention in Miami and certainly bringing a present for his "best girl" (Sissy) with him, and slipping out of her bed in her cute, little nightgown and going through the bathroom to open the door into her mother's room (probably hurrying because of the slight chill in the air) and gleefully and happily planning to slip into bed with her warm and sleeping "Mommy" (while Daddy was away and Mommy was all alone) and maybe even doing just that.

And encountering cold and unresponsive flesh!

A murdered mother.

A mother who would never again turn slowly to her in the warm bed and welcome her with soft arms and murmured assurances of maternal love which were so much a real part of Sissy's life.

Shuddering, Leroy Smith had firmly closed the hallway door into Sissy's room and backtracked to the Scene of the Crime.

Here, it had been almost as difficult for the impressionable young man. Thank God, they had removed the body before he arrived. He was spared that, though his imagination could place the naked and murdered body of Ellie Blake squarely in the middle of the big nuptial bed in front of him.

All of the top covers were thrown back, and the bottom sheet was fitted tightly at the corners. Certainly, there was no indication of a struggle in the room. Beside the bed in disarray lay Ellie's clothing. At least, he supposed they were the clothes Ellie Blake had worn before retiring last night. He wondered if she generally tossed them aside carelessly on the floor when she went to bed at night.

Probably not, he thought. Not on a normal night when her husband was there and they decorously went to bed together. But last night she had been alone in the house. Her husband was in Miami and maybe she had luxuriated in being alone and just wantonly tossed aside her clothes before getting into bed naked and alone.

What kind of woman had she been, really, he wondered. Did a married woman get sick and tired of going to bed decorously every night with the same man? Had Ellie Blake been happy to have those few days alone in the house (with only her six-year-old daughter) while her husband was in Miami?

It seemed to him that this bedroom should be able to tell him something. Murder had been committed here less than twelve hours before. Murder most foul. There should be *something* here for a Trained Investigator to get his teeth into.

That was when he heard an automobile coming up the drive and stopping in front of the house.

He crossed the bedroom swiftly to the window and looked down. He didn't recognize the shabby coupé parked outside the front door or the gangling figure that got out of the driver's seat and walked briskly around the front of the car toward the front door.

He hurried out and down the stairs and was two steps from the bottom when the chimes rang in the living room to his left. They sounded loud in the empty and silent house and a queer sort of tingle raced up and down his spine, and he sternly disregarded it as he went to the front door and pulled it open.

A tall man with thin features and cavernous eyes confronted him. He had alertly intelligent eyes and seemed perfectly self-assured as he looked at the young man in uniform and murmured, "Officer Smith? I'm the Press. Miami *News*."

It was the first time Leroy had ever been addressed as

"Officer Smith." It was also the first time he had ever actually encountered a reporter from a big city newspaper. In a shaking voice, he said,

"Yes. I'm . . . Leroy Smith. Officer Leroy Smith," he amended, getting some of the shakiness out of his voice.

"Rourke." Timothy Rourke held out a thin hand and winced as the young man wrung it with unnecessary vigor. "Your chief of police said you were in charge here, and suggested I get a statement from you."

"For the . . . Miami *News*? Say, you're Timothy Rourke, aren't you? I read your by-lined stories all the time in the paper. You want a statement from me?"

"Whatever information you're at liberty to make public," Rourke told him urbanely. "I got the impression from Chief Jenson that he fully expects you to come up with a solution to the murder."

"Well, I don't know about that," Smith disclaimed half-heartedly. "I do have a few ideas, I guess. Come on in the house, Mr. Rourke. You want to go up to the bedroom where they found her?"

"Let's look around down here first." Rourke walked into the hallway and glanced through the door into the neat kitchen, and then into the living room on the right. "Is that the window where you think entry was made?"

"It was found unlocked and open a couple of inches. Everything else locked up tight. No fingerprints, though, and no foreign substances picked up from the floor inside by the special filter on my vacuum cleaner . . . so the findings are inconclusive. But there's these two highball glasses in front of the sofa, Mr. Rourke. Fingerprints on one glass

I've identified as belonging to the deceased . . . I don't know about the others."

"You mean she sat here and had a drink with someone before she got herself strangled?"

"Well, I . . . I guess she had a drink with someone all right. Don't quote me as saying I think it was her murderer, though. More likely an innocent friend."

"But you've photographed the prints just in case?" insisted Rourke.

The young policeman colored slightly. "I don't have a proper fingerprint camera. But I did lift the prints with scotch tape and I have them for identification."

"Excellent." Rourke nodded emphatically and the young man glowed. The reported jotted down some notes on a wad of copy paper. "Leroy Smith. Is that right?"

"That's right. I was all prepared to make a moulage of any footprints outside the window, you could say in your newspaper story if you want, but unfortunately it's all gravel outside as you can see for yourself if you look."

Rourke nodded absently and went back to the stairway after a last glance around the neat living room. "Upstairs, eh?"

"The room to the right at the head of the stairs." Smith followed him up eagerly. "The other bedroom with connecting bath is their little girl's room. Only six years old and she was sound asleep all the time. Didn't know a thing until she woke up this morning and went to call her mother and found her lying there, in the middle of the bed, cold and dead. It makes me sick to think of it."

"Had she been screwed?" Rourke asked callously as he

stepped inside the bedroom and looked at the wide, smooth bed.

"I . . . I . . . don't know," stammered Leroy Smith behind him. "I didn't even see her body, and I don't know how one would determine a thing like that."

"Any semen stains on the bed? You used ultraviolet, didn't you? Or don't you know . . . ?"

"I am perfectly aware," said the young man stiffly, "that an ultraviolet light will cause the stains of semen and other physiological fluids to re-emit energy in the form of visible light generally known as *fluorescence*. Semen, indeed," he went on didactically to cover an inward confusion, "will generally show a rather bright, blue-white fluorescence. Unfortunately, though, we have no ultra-violet equipment on hand."

Rourke shrugged and crossed the room to a large dressing table. "The doctor should be able to tell us that." He picked up a double cardboard-framed photograph of a smiling man and a very attractive, calm-faced woman and studied it. "Is this a picture of the Blakes?"

Leroy Smith glanced at it and nodded. "Taken when they were married, I guess. Marvin looks just about the same today, but Ellie is . . . was . . . a lot prettier today than then."

Rourke nodded slowly and closed the cardboard folder and tucked it under his arm. "I can use this in the paper." He strode across the room to enter the bathroom and look around, then opened the door on the other side and glanced into Sissy's room.

When he returned, Leroy Smith said hesitantly, "If you

think you'd like a picture of me, Mr. Rourke, to run in the newspaper, I could get you one without any trouble just by stopping off at home for a minute. It shows me in my uniform and all."

"Just exactly what I need," Rourke told him enthusiastically. "We'll caption it: Scientific Sleuth Goes Clueless." He started briskly out of the room. "Now then: Tell me how to get to the Wilsson house. I understand that's where the Blake child is staying until her father gets home from Miami this afternoon."

"That's right." Leroy Smith hurried after him. "You go down to the end of this lane and turn to the right . . . ."

8

In even the most ordinary circumstances Minerva Wilsson was an exceedingly voluble woman. Most of her friends indulgently agreed that she could talk more and say less than any woman in seven counties, and one homespun philosopher had opined sagely, "You just got to take part of what Minerva says with a grain of salt. It stands to reason there just ain't that much truth in the world."

That was in the most ordinary circumstances.

Today, of course, the circumstances were most extraordinary, and by eleven o'clock in the morning Minerva had broken all her own previous records for long-distance gabbing. Since seven o'clock when the news had begun to spread, her telephone had rung incessantly, and there had been a constant stream of callers to the Wilsson bungalow.

If she had told it once she had told it forty times, each

time with certain added dramatic highlights and embellishments which made for better listening and drew more gushing "ohs" and "ahs" and "do tells."

"Right after six o'clock it was when the telephone started ringing and woke me spang up out of the soundest sleep I'd had all night. I just knew it was terrible news. Like a premonition, I guess you'd say. I've always been real sensitive like that, you know, ever since I was little. It was like it wasn't the telephone at all, but the shrill screaming of a soul in deadly agony that woke me up. But I was out of bed and on my feet before I had time to think, and Harry just lying there on his back snoring peacefully through it all.

"Well, I tell you I just flew into the other room and grabbed up the telephone and said hello, and then I heard this tiny, little voice that seemed like it came from a far distance off, almost like it wasn't real but came from some place not on this earth.

"And it said 'Aunt Minerva', and it was like it was crying but not quite crying either, but choked up and frightened and, well . . . *tragic*, that's what it was. I can tell you it gave me a turn. I wasn't quite all awake, I guess, and it was like it was part of a dream, but I knew I wasn't *dreaming*. I remember standing there and distinctly thinking to myself, 'I wish it was a dream, but I know it isn't,' and then this little voice said, 'This is Sissy, Aunt Minerva. Mommy's hurt bad. She's sick, I guess. She's lying in bed and won't talk to me.' That poor, dear lamb. Can you imagine?

"And I *knew* right then. I tell you I felt it in my bones. Don't ask me how. I'm just psychic, I guess. And I said, 'You stay right there downstairs to open the front door and let me in, Sissy,' and then I hung up the phone and scooted back to the bedroom and didn't even take time to get dressed, but put on my slippers and a robe, and Harry sort of woke up and rolled over to look at me and he asked, half-asleep, 'Was that the telephone?' And I said to him, 'That's what it was, all right. It's Ellie Blake. She's dead, Harry.' That's exactly what I said to him, right out, without any ifs or ands or buts. Don't ask me how I knew, but I did. And I said, 'You get up and put on a pot of coffee. I'm going over to bring Sissy back home with me,' because I remembered that Marvin was at that convention in Miami and wouldn't be home until this afternoon and there was that poor child all alone, and I ran out the back door in my robe and slippers and drove as fast as I could to the Blake house, and there was dear, little Sissy, standing in the front door like I'd told her, bare-footed and in her little nightgown with her face all screwed up trying not to cry and her great, big eyes pleading with me, it looked like, to wake her mamma up and tell her it wasn't so.

"I just dropped down to my knees there on the doorstep and held out my arms to her, thinking to myself, but not saying it out loud, 'You poor, motherless lamb, you,' and she flung her arms around my neck and pressed her face up against me, but not a word out of her and not a tear in those sweet, big eyes.

"And I carried her inside and put her down gentle-like in the living room, and I said as brisk and businesslike as could be, 'You stay right here, honey, while Aunt Minerva goes up and sees about your mamma.'

"And she stood there and she looked at me, sad-like and

understanding 'way beyond her years, and she folded her little hands in front of her and she said, 'Mommy's dead, isn't she, Aunt Minerva? God took her up to heaven in the night last night while I was asleep, didn't He?'

"Well, I tell you it was all I could do to keep from bursting right out and crying my own self, but I said, 'You just let me go up and see,' and I turned away and went up the stairs, dragging my feet and slow because something just *told* me what I was going to find when I got up there.

"Poor Ellie! She *has* been running to fat this last year, you know that, and there she lay. Lumpy and shapeless, you might say. Right in the middle of that big bed without a stitch to cover up her nakedness, and those terrible black and blue bruises all around her throat and her tongue hanging out, all blue and swollen, and her eyes open and staring like they'd looked down into the bottomless pit of hell before Death mercifully drew the veil over whatever it was she looked at before she died.

"And you knew right then that some vile man-creature had had his way with her before he choked the life out of her. The way she was twisted up like her limbs had been writhing and she'd fought him off as best she could.

"Because you can say what you will about Ellie Blake, but you know mighty well she was a fine, Christian woman in every respect, and maybe she was considered sort of fast and loose when she was in high school and all, but, after she and Marv started going steady and certainly after they got married and had Sissy, there's nobody can say she ever looked at another man.

"You mark my words, and I guess I was closer to Ellie

than any other woman friend in the whole of Sunray Beach, you'll find out it was pure rape, that's what it was. Some man that got the wrong sort of ideas about Ellie because she was so friendly and it wasn't her fault if the good Lord gave her a pair of hips that twitched from behind whenever she walked down the street. It wasn't that Ellie *intended* it that way. Not the way I see it. She did like to attract attention from the men, maybe, and many's the time I've kidded Harry when I saw his eyes sort of bugging out when Ellie walked past, but shucks, Harry knew right well, just like every other man in town, that Ellie didn't *mean* anything by it.

"I knew right off there wasn't anything I could do, and I never even went into the room. All I could think about was that poor motherless lamb downstairs and how I had to get her away where she wouldn't have to see Ellie again, and about Marvin, poor soul, having himself a good time in Miami at the convention without ever dreaming what he was going to come home to.

"So I went on into Sissy's room and grabbed some clothes for her and then I hurried back downstairs and there she was standing right there in the doorway to the living room where I'd left her, and still not a tear on her cheeks. And she looked at me with those big eyes that seemed like she knew everything, and she said, 'She is dead, isn't she, Aunt Minerva?' and I lied to her. I said, 'Land's sake, child, how can we tell till we get a doctor?' and I pushed the bundle of clothes into her arms and went past her to the telephone and called Doctor Higgens and woke him up out of bed and told him to get over there fast, and then I called Police

Chief Ollie Jenson at his home and woke him up, and I said into the telephone, real low so Sissy wouldn't hear me, standing back in the doorway like she was, I said:

" 'I'm at Ellie Blake's house and she's been murdered and raped in the night.' That's just what I said to him, right out. 'Murdered and raped,' I said. 'And you better get over here. I called Doctor Higgens,' I said, 'though Lord knows there's nothing he can do for poor Ellie now, and I'm taking the little girl home with me.'

"And I hung up fast and turned back to Sissy and she was looking at me with the strangest look on her face and she asked, 'What's raped, Aunt Minerva?' Well! You can imagine. You could have knocked me over with a feather. I never *thought* she could hear me. What *could* I say to the poor lamb? So I just pretended I didn't know what she was talking about, and I bundled her up in my arms and carried her out to the car and brought her straight on home with me, and I put her right to bed in the spare bedroom, and that's where she is right now. She doesn't say a word and she hasn't cried a single tear yet, just lies on her back staring up at the ceiling and she doesn't want anything to eat or drink. I asked Doctor Higgens, but he said it was best just to leave her alone. Let the shock wear off, you know.

"Well, say now, there's a car pulling up in the driveway and I don't know who it is. Some man getting out and coming to the door. A strange man. I'd better hang up and go see."

It was Timothy Rourke at the door. He was confronted by a small, birdlike woman with a sharp nose and very bright eyes and a fluttery manner. She said yes she was Mrs. Harry Wilsson, and, yes, she guessed she and Harry were about the closest friends the Blakes had in town, and oh, was he really a reporter from the Miami paper ... "well come right on in and sit down and I'll try to tell you anything I can."

The gangling reporter followed her into a small and painfully neat sitting room where the outer shades were drawn to give the room a funereal atmosphere, and he perched uncomfortably on the edge of a hard sofa and looked about the room unhappily for an ashtray without seeing one, and Minerva sat down opposite him and drew in a deep breath and leaned forward and began, "I guess you've heard that I was the first one over to the Blake house this morning and that I found the body as you might say, and. . . ."

"Yes, I know that, Mrs. Wilsson," Rourke interrupted her, pretending to glance down at some scribbled notes in his hand. "And I believe you brought the little girl home with you and are keeping her here until her father returns from Miami this afternoon. How is she taking it?"

"She just doesn't seem to realize it at all, Mr. Rourke. You did say that was your name, didn't you? It's a mercy, I guess, that she doesn't. So young and all. It was a terrible shock for her, you see. Alone there in the house and all, and waking up this morning so happy and innocent and going into her mother's room, and what did she see. . . .?"

Rourke said, "Naturally it was a shock. But kids of that age are pretty resilient in my experience. They often understand a great deal more than we give them credit for. She didn't hear anything during the night?"

"Not a single thing, I guess. She's always been a very sound sleeper. Ever since she was a tiny thing. Always went right to bed without any fuss, and straight off to sleep. Harry and I have been there lots of evenings for bridge, and I always said Sissy was the *best* thing the way she went to sleep without wanting a light left on or a drink of water or anything the way so many children do. But Ellie had trained her real good, and I always say. . . ."

"Could I see her for a moment, Mrs. Wilsson." Rourke got to his feet firmly. "I won't upset her or disturb her. I'd like to be able to describe her to my readers."

"Well, of *course*. If you're in a terrible hurry. I thought you'd want an eye-witness account. . . ."

"I'd like to come back later when I have more time . . . and maybe get a tape recording. Right now I have to telephone in a story very shortly. If I could just see the little girl. . . ."

"Right back this way." Minerva went out of the sitting room and preceded him on tiptoes down a hallway to a closed door leading into a back bedroom. She paused with her hand on the knob, turned to Rourke with a finger pressed against her lips, and then turned the knob soundlessly and pushed the door open.

Bright sunlight streamed in through an open window and glistened on the tousled, golden hair of Sissy Blake, who sat upright and cross-legged in the center of the bed and regarded them gravely.

Minerva said, "I see you're wide awake, Sissy. I thought you might be asleep. I left the shade down. . . ."

"I let it up to let the sunshine in," said Sissy. She had smooth, regular features and big, violet eyes. "Do I have to stay here in bed all day? Why can't I go to school, Aunt Minerva?"

"Not today, dear. Your daddy will be coming home this afternoon and you want to be all fresh and rested to meet him. Here's a man that's come all the way from Miami to see you, Sissy. He's a nice man from the newspaper, and. . . ."

The telephone began shrilling in the sitting room, and Minerva straightened up and glanced down the hall hesitantly.

Timothy Rourke took advantage of the moment to take her arm firmly and push her out the door. "You'd better answer your phone, Mrs. Wilsson. I'll talk to Sissy just a minute."

"Well, if you're sure. . . ."

Rourke said, "I'm sure," and closed the door between them. He turned with his back against the door and grinned at the little girl seated in the middle of the bed and said, "Hi, Sissy."

She said, "Hi. What's your name?" She regarded him with grave curiosity and with no trace of nervousness.

He said, "Timothy," and took two steps to the end of the bed and sat down on one corner of it.

She said, "Did you know my mommy was dead?"

Rourke cleared his troat and said, "I know, Sissy. I'm very sorry."

"I'm sorry too. And Daddy will be sorry when he comes home from Miami."

"I know he will. Tell me about last night, Sissy. You and your mother were alone. Did you sleep all night without waking up?"

"After I went to sleep I did. But Mommy wasn't alone when I went to sleep. Uncle Harry was there."

Rourke steeled himself against any show of surprise. "You mean Mr. Wilsson?"

"Yes. He's the only Uncle Harry I've got. First I thought I'd stay awake until Mommy came to bed and then maybe I'd slip in with her because she doesn't mind when Daddy's away. Then I heard them talking downstairs and I got up and looked down the stairs and saw Uncle Harry coming out of the kitchen with two glasses in his hand, and Mommy doesn't like it when I don't go right to sleep if there's company and so I went back to bed and pretty soon I went to sleep. Did Mommy hurt when she died, Mr. Timothy?"

"I don't think so, Sissy." Rourke's mouth was dry and his heart was pounding. He heard Minerva coming down the hall and he got up hastily and leaned over to touch the tips of fingers to Sissy's brow. "I have to go now. You be a good girl and rest until your daddy comes home."

The door opened and Rourke went past Minerva into the hall saying hastily, "Thanks a lot, Mrs. Wilsson. I'll have to. . . ."

"Maybe you'd like a cup of coffee, Mr. Rourke. I've got a pot fresh made. And then I could tell you a couple of things I've thought of that might be important, me knowing Ellie so well and all. More like sisters, we were. Harry and Marvin, too, for that matter. The four of us were always just as close as could be."

Rourke said through his teeth, "I'm sure you were, Mrs. Wilsson. But you'll have to excuse me for now. I've got to get to a telephone to meet a deadline."

He hurried on ahead of her and escaped through the open front door while a flow of conversation continued unabated behind him.

My God, he thought, my God! Out of the mouths of babes. It was, he realized, the merest chance that had led Sissy to mention the presence of Harry Wilsson at the house last evening. It meant absolutely nothing to the child. It had no importance whatsoever in her mind. It was like that classic story about the Invisible Man who committed the murder. The postman on his rounds. Although he had been seen by a dozen witnesses, not one of them *knew* they had seen him. He was just part of the landscape.

Like Uncle Harry in Sissy's mind. He was always around, wasn't he? Often in the evenings when she was sent to bed while the foursome had drinks and played bridge in the living room.

There was no difference in the mind of a six-year-old between his being there last night alone with her mother and the other times when the four of them were there together. He was certain she hadn't mentioned it to Minerva this morning, and it was a lead pipe cinch that Harry hadn't reported to his wife that he had dropped in on Ellie Blake in her husband's absence the preceding evening to have a drink with her.

Innocent enough, probably. But, if it were all that innocent, why hadn't Harry spoken right up this morning as soon as he learned what happened to Ellie in the night?

He evidently did not realize that Sissy had seen him from the top of the stairs. The way she told it so innocently, she had been tucked away in her own bed by her mother before Harry arrived, and neither one of them had been aware that she had gotten up and peeked down at them. This morning, Harry Wilsson must feel that his secret was perfectly safe, whether the visit had been entirely innocent or not. Either way he'd see no reason to come forward and offer gratuitous information and get himself involved in a murder investigation. That didn't mean the man was guilty of anything . . . even of an innocent flirtation with his best friend's well-stacked wife.

Rourke looked at his watch as he drove away from the Wilsson house and noted that almost an hour had elapsed since he had telephoned the redheaded private detective in Miami. It was still too early to buy a drink, so Rourke drove directly to the motel where he still had a key to the room he had occupied the night before.

His bag was still there and the room had not been made up. Rourke sat on the edge of the rumpled bed and gave the switchboard operator Shayne's office number in Miami and told her to charge the call to his room, remarking that he would be staying over at least another day.

Lucy Hamilton's lilting voice came over the wire first from Miami, and when Rourke said, "Good morning, doll," she said, "Michael just came back, Tim. I'll put him on." There was a click and a moment of silence, and then Shayne's voice:

"Pretty much of a wild goose chase, Tim. I talked to some of the delegates at the hotel, and several of them know

Marvin Blake personally, but they were all nursing hang-overs and didn't remember too much about last night. It was one of those free-for-alls, I gather, small-town boys having a wild night out in the big city. A pornographic movie and liquor flowing all over the place. Your man did check out yesterday. Just before four o'clock, without telling anyone or giving any explanation it appears. Paid his hotel bill in cash and just walked out. I did find the bellboy who brought his bag down. He remembered it because it was funny for a delegate to be checking out before the convention was over, and by chance he happened to notice that Blake ducked into a rather expensive gift shop next door and made a purchase. I checked that out as best I could with a rather vague description of Blake, and I believe he bought a twenty-eight-dollar pair of earrings which he had gift wrapped. Nobody remembers seeing him around the hotel after that, but that doesn't mean he mayn't have been there for the high-jinks."

Shayne paused and Timothy Rourke took a moment to digest this information, and Shayne asked, "Does that help any?"

"I don't know how it fits in, Mike. Look, I'm getting in over my depth up here. Are you tied up on anything important?"

"Nothing I can't walk away from for a couple of days."

"Then you're retained by the *News*, Mike. Jump in your car and get up here, huh? I'll be at the Sunray Beach Motel or leave a message. It's about a three-hour drive. If you leave right away you should be here in plenty of time to join me as a welcoming party for Marvin Blake if he does arrive on that afternoon train he's expected on."

Michael Shayne was not one to waste time with unnecessary questions. He said, "I'll see you, Tim," and hung up.

Rourke broke the connection and got the motel switchboard again. This time he made it a person-to-person call to his City Editor at the *News*. When he got through, he said swiftly, "Tim Rourke in Sunray Beach, Cal. I ran into a real juicy murder here, and stayed over."

"Sunray Beach? Woman named Ellie Blake strangled in her bed while her husband attends convention in Miami? We got a first lead over the wire."

"Right. Nude body and all. Discovered by her six-year-old daughter early this morning. No clues. Here's your headline, Cal. News offers thousand-dollar reward in Blake murder and retains famed Miami sleuth to assist local police in solving case. You can fill in the rest."

"Wait . . . a . . . little . . . minute. Is it really that good?"

"I got a feeling in my bones, Cal. I just talked to Mike Shayne and he's already on his way up. Play it my way, huh? Chances are Mike and I'll solve it and save you the reward. But get moving fast to hit the late edition."

"If you say so, Tim. I'll have to get an okay . . ."

"Make up your headline first," Rourke advised him blithely, "and then get your front office okay. I'll be back to you later on this afternoon."

He hung up and looked at his watch again. It was not yet noon. Still too early to buy a drink in Sunray Beach. He opened the telephone directory and looked up the address of Doctor Higgens.

9

The doctor's office was one of several ground-floor suites arranged around three sides of pleasant, palm-bordered courtyard with colorful flowerbeds and a fountain in the center of it. It was entered from the street through an archway bearing the inscription, *Sunray Medical Center*, with plaques on either side giving the names of the doctors and dentists who were conveniently grouped inside.

Timothy Rourke found a sign indicating Doctor Higgens' office on the second door from the archway on the right. He entered a pleasant waiting room with comfortable chairs and smoking stands ranged against two walls and a desk at the far end with a pert young lady in nurse's uniform sitting behind it. She was the only occupant of the waiting room, and she looked up with a bright smile as the reporter advanced to the front of her desk.

"Doctor's office hours are from one to four," she told him, studying his face with frank curiosity.

Rourke said, "I don't want to see him professionally. That is, I haven't got anything the matter with me."

She said, "Oh?" as though she doubted that statement, and waited for him to go on.

Rourke smiled his nicest smile and eased his left hip down onto a corner of the wide, bare desk in front of the girl. "I'm a reporter on the Miami *News*," he confided to her, "and I'd like to get some information from the doctor about the woman who was murdered last night. Was she a regular patient of his?"

"Oh, yes. Wasn't that an awful thing to happen? She was in just a couple of weeks ago with her little girl. She's a real, living doll . . . Sissy, I mean," she added in some confusion. "When I think about her . . . *finding* her mother like that this morning, it makes me want to cry."

"Go ahead," Rourke said. He got a limp cigarette out of his pocket and put it between his lips and fumbled for a match.

"What?"

"Cry," Rourke told her gently, putting flame to the end of the cigarette and drawing in deeply. "Then I'll put you in my story," he went on in a tone that was half-bantering, half-serious. "With a picture," he added enthusiastically. "It's always a good idea to inject some good, healthy sex appeal in a rape murder story."

She said, "Oh, you!" and wrinkled up her nose at him, and then asked in a low, hesitant voice, "Was she . . . raped?"

Rourke said, "I'm hoping the doctor will tell me that. I understand he's doing the autopsy. Do you know if he's completed it?"

"I guess he has." She bit her under-lip and looked embarrassed for some reason. "He came back from the hospital a little while ago."

"Do you suppose I could see him for a minute?"

"I'll see." She got up and went through a door behind her desk, closing it carefully behind her, and Rourke sat on the corner of her desk and swung one leg lazily and wondered if it was worthwhile trying to make a date with her that evening.

She came back through the door after a moment and held it open invitingly and said, "Doctor can see you for a few minutes, but he has an important appointment at twelve."

"So have I," Rourke told her with a wide grin. "With a tall glass of bourbon and branch water as soon as the local bistro opens its reluctant doors." He went past her into a brightly-lighted consultation room where a tall, white-haired man with very bright, very blue eyes regarded him without noticeable pleasure and said flatly, "I don't want to waste your time, young man, nor my own. I have no intention of discussing one of my patients with a representative of the press." The sour emphasis he put on the final word made it sound like an obscenity.

Rourke said, "Ex-patient, Doctor. Ellie Blake has become news, whether you like it or not. I won't quote you if you prefer not, but I would like to get my dope from the horse's mouth instead of having to pick it up in bits and pieces and rumors from around town."

"I do definitely prefer not to be quoted. Now, what is it you want to know?"

Timothy Rourke sat in a straight chair and got out a pencil and some copy paper and matched the doctor's own cold, impersonal tone.

"What do you make the time of death?"

"Between ten P.M. and two A.M."

"And the cause?"

"Manual strangulation."

"By a strong man?"

"That is a matter for conjecture. It wasn't accomplished by a weakling."

"Did she struggle much?"

"As much as any woman could, I presume, with a man's hands throttling her. You know this isn't a proper subject for medical testimony, Mr. Rourke."

"I'm trying to get a picture. Was she undressed before or after she was murdered?"

"How on earth would I know a thing like that?"

"Had she been sexually attacked?"

"Exactly what does that euphemism mean to you . . . and your readers?" the doctor demanded disagreeably.

Rourke looked up guilelessly. "All right. We'll skip the euphemisms. Was she raped?"

"I can't say. She was a mature married woman with a six-year-old daughter. There are no definite outward signs of rape, but that signifies nothing."

"Had she had sexual intercourse?"

"There was a quantity of fresh seminal fluid with live spermatozoa in the vaginal passage," the doctor informed him drily.

"You took samples, Doctor?"

"I made several slides from smears obtained from the interior of the vagina."

"Did you test for blood-grouping to possibly identify the source?"

"I did not," snapped Doctor Higgens. "Perhaps you labor under the delusion of many laymen that all pro-teinaceous body fluids carry the same isoagglutinogens found in the blood corpuscles. In some cases this is true, but often it is not the case."

"Are you saying, Doctor, that seminal fluid cannot be tested to indicate the blood group of the man who pro-duced it?"

"In some instances it can. Often it cannot."

"And you haven't determined which is which in this case?"

"I have not yet done so."

Rourke shrugged and tapped the end of his pencil against his teeth. "I'm a layman, of course, but I have covered a lot of crimes and it has been my understanding that semen can be typed the same as blood. How about this, Doctor? I've also been told that the spermatozoa themselves can be identified under a high-power microscope as having come from a certain individual. That they have definite charac-teristics that are identifiable. Is that not true?"

Doctor Higgens made a tent out of his ten fingers and peered over the top of it at the reporter with an irritable frown. "I haven't the time to give you a classroom lecture on the subject. Nor the inclination." He hesitated and then went on stiffly, "There are some indications that the morphology of spermatozoa may be characteristic of the individual . . . and can be positively identified by a highly trained technician in that field."

Timothy Rourke shrugged and dropped the subject, which he felt was getting beyond him. "Did you test the victim for alcohol in the blood?"

"I did. With the generally inconclusive results that are normal with such tests. It is my opinion that Mrs. Blake had had from one to three drinks following dinner."

"Then she wasn't drunk?"

Doctor Higgens shrugged and stood up. "That is a completely relative term. A matter of semantics. And also a matter of the individual capacity to absorb and carry alcohol. Mrs. Blake was not a drinking woman. It is impossible for me to form any opinion of the effects one to three drinks might have had on her following dinner." He paused and looked at his watch pointedly. "And now, if you don't mind, I have an apopintment."

Rourke said blithely, "I don't mind at all. And thanks." He thrust the copy paper in his pocket and went out.

10

Dave's Bar and Grill—Package Liquor was on Main Street just past the City Hall where Mabel Handel had told him it would be. Rourke found a parking slot just beyond, and glanced at his watch as he strolled back to the entrance. It lacked five minutes of twelve o'clock, but the door was invitingly open and Rourke went in hopefully.

There was a short bar on the left and half a dozen tables in the small room that was partitioned off from the dining room with an archway between the two. At the end of the bar there were shelves of bottled goods with an iron lattice-work drawn across the front of them and secured with a padlock.

There were no customers, but there was a slight, sandy-haired man wearing a fresh white jacket polishing glasses behind the bar.

He looked at Rourke curiously as the reporter seated himself at the far end of the bar, nodded amiably and said, "Morning," giving an extra flourish to the glass in his hands.

Rourke said sadly, "If it's still morning I suppose that's too early to get a drink."

"Well, sir." The bartender turned and craned his neck to look up at the big clock behind the bar. The big hand was two minutes short of twelve. "I reckon that clock of mine could be a couple minutes slow. What's your pleasure?"

"Bourbon. Make it a double shot just to celebrate the beginning of a new day. With a little water but don't drown it."

The bartender made his drink, splashing in extra whiskey to give it a good dark color, and set it in front of him. "Stranger in town?"

Rourke took a long experimental drink and smacked his lips. "I'll probably be sticking around a day or so . . . on account of that murder you had last night."

"Terrible thing, wasn't it? Mighty fine woman. First time anything like that ever happened in Sunray Beach, I can tell you. Gives the town a bad name. Say you're here on account of it? State police, or like that?"

"Reporter," Rourke told him. "Miami *News*. We're offering a thousand-dollar reward for pertinent information."

"Is that a fact? Well, I sure hope you get to pay out that reward money, Mister. Man that'd do a thing like that just isn't human, the way I look at it. I'll help string him up my own self when they catch him. Some damned hobo, you can be sure of that. Marvin and Ellie Blake was mighty well liked here in Sunray. I guess you might say there wasn't a better-respected woman in town. Hanging's too good for a bastard'd do a thing like that. Oughtta string him up by the balls and set a slow fire going underneath him."

Rourke nodded soberly and said, "It was a mighty nasty thing. Tough on the little girl. The husband, too."

"It'll just about finish up old Marv. God! Think about coming home to that. After being off on a convention and all. He just about worshipped the ground his wife and little Sissy walked on, Marv did. I'm telling you I'd hate to be the man to meet that train this afternoon and tell Marv the news."

"You mean he hasn't been notified yet?"

"I reckon not. I was talking down the street in the drug store a little while ago and one of the fellows there had just been talking to Ollie Jenson . . . he's Chief of Police here . . . and Ollie said he didn't see any good in breaking the bad news to him till he had to. Stands to reason there's nothing Marv can do about it. Bad enough when he does get home and has to find out."

A party of three men entered the front door and seated themselves on stools. The sandy-haired man bustled to them and took their orders, and Rourke turned his head to watch them idly over the rim of his glass.

As the bartender set drinks in front of them, he leaned forward and spoke rapidly in a low voice, and all three of them turned their heads simultaneously to look at Rourke.

He blandly disregarded their interest, emptied his glass thirstily and set it down. When the bartender approached him again, he said, "I'd like another. Better make it a single this time."

The bartender set it in front of him and said, "One of those fellows there is Harry Wilsson. He and his wife were about the closest friends the Blakes had in town, and Harry's taking it mighty hard. Mrs. Wilsson's the first one Sissy Blake telephoned to this morning after she woke up and found her mamma choked to death in bed, and she went right over there without stopping to get dressed and called the police and Doctor Higgens. They got Sissy at their house now, until Marvin gets back anyhow."

Rourke took a sip of his drink and glanced at the three men. "Which one is Wilsson?"

"One on this end."

The man seated nearest to Rourke was in his early thirties, tall and well-built, with carefully-combed, glossy black hair and a somewhat bushy black mustache. He was drinking whiskey, Rourke noted, straight from a shot-glass, with a small beer as a chaser.

Rourke nodded and said, "Thanks." Then he looked at the still locked supply of bottled liquor at the end of the bar, and asked, "Do you sell stuff by the bottle?"

"To take out, yeh. I just haven't got around to opening it up yet."

"Let me have a pint. Four Roses, I guess."

The bartender got a key from a hook behind him, unlocked the padlock and pushed the iron lattice back. He put a pint bottle in a brown paper sack and set it on the bar beside the reporter.

Rourke slid it into the side pocket of his coat, then got

off his stool and with his drink in hand approached Harry Wilsson.

The man jerked around nervously when Rourke stopped beside him and asked, "Mr. Wilsson?"

He had very black eyes and full, almost pouting, lips beneath the heavy mustache. He said, very quickly, "That's right," and wet his lips nervously and glanced away.

The reporter said, "My name is Rourke . . . from the Miami *News*. I'm in town covering the Blake murder, and I wonder if you could spare me a few minutes."

"I guess so," Wilsson said huskily. He gave a little self-conscious laugh that turned out to be more of a snort. "Don't know what I can tell you, though, except I'm mighty well broken up about it."

"I understand you were close friends," Rourke said sympathetically. "Why don't you bring your drink and let's go back to a table where we can talk a moment?" He turned and led the way to the farthest table in the rear, and Harry Wilsson followed him, carrying his half-emptied shot-glass in one hand and beer in the other.

Rourke took a chair and Wilsson sat down opposite him, grimacing and shaking his head slowly. "I just can't get it through my head. I keep thinking about Marvin. How I would feel if a thing like that happened to my wife while I was off raising hell at a convention?" He closed his fingers tightly about his shot-glass, lifted it to his mouth convulsively and tossed off the remainder of the whiskey.

Rourke said sententiously, "It's always hardest on those who are left behind. Have you got any idea who might have done it, Mr. Wilsson?"

"God, no! How could I? No one who knew them, certainly. Nobody in this town. It had to be a transient. Chief Jenson says he must have got into the house through the front window that was left unlocked. I told Ellie to lock up carefully while Marvin was gone, but she just laughed at me. Nobody does lock up in Sunray, hardly. First time anything like this ever happened."

"When did you see her last?" Rourke asked smoothly. "I suppose you dropped in and more or less looked after things while her husband was away . . . being such close friends."

"Well, Ellie knew she could call on me for anything she needed. But she was pretty independent that way. She stopped by the house yesterday afternoon with Sissy and that was the last time we saw her alive. We talked about Marv being at the convention and all, and I kidded her about how he was probably stepping out on her with some of those fancy city women, and she just kidded right back about how she didn't worry about Marv in Miami. She didn't come right out and say it, you know, but she practically said that old Marv knew he had something a lot better waiting for him right there at home than he was going to get from any woman in Miami. And then . . . oh, God!" Harry Wilsson groaned and spread out his hands and then ran his fingers through his glossy, black hair distractedly. "When you think about last night, and her up in her bedroom and sleeping there naked and dreaming, maybe, about Marv. . . ." He groaned again and put the spread fingers of both hands over his face.

Rourke settled back in his chair and reached down to the

paper sack in his coat pocket containing the pint of Four Roses and wriggled the mouth of the sack open in his pocket, and said, "Then that's the last thing either you or your wife saw of her . . . when she stopped by your place late yesterday afternoon? Just for the record, I guess maybe that's the last anyone saw of her alive?"

"I guess so." Harry Wilsson took his hands away from his face and showed a strained and pain-racked countenance to the reporter. "Except Sissy, of course. And . . . whoever did it."

Rourke nodded and emptied his glass. He glanced over his shoulder and saw that more customers had entered the bar and the bartender was busy serving them. He pushed back his chair and got up with his empty glass in his left hand, and said, "I'll get us a refill. What are you drinking?"

"Bourbon. All right, just a shot. I've got plenty of beer."

Rourke nodded and put his right hand over the empty shot-glass on the table. He slid his first two fingers inside the glass and stretched them apart to lift the glass without touching the outside of it, and turned away quickly, transferring the glass to the paper sack inside his pocket and dropping it gently atop the pint of whiskey as he moved toward the end of the bar.

There, he caught the bartender's attention and pushed his own glass forward, ordering, "Another single with branch water for me, and another slug of straight stuff for Mr. Wilsson."

He got out his wallet and extracted a twenty while his drink was being made, and he pushed it across the mahogany when his drink and a full shot-glass were placed in front of him. He said, "Take them all out of that . . . not for-getting the pint," and he waited to get his change and left a dollar on the bar when he went back and sat down again in front of Harry Wilsson.

He pushed the man's drink in front of him, and tilted his own glass up. He drank half of it and smacked his lips happily and said, "I never saw her, of course, but they tell me Ellie Blake was quite a piece. What I mean is," he went on hastily, seeing storm signals in Wilsson's black eyes, "she was the sort of woman that gave a man ideas about her whether she meant it or not. Which might, in a sense, explain what happened to her last night. Because some man got horny just looking at her."

"Ellie did have a way about her," said Wilsson brood-ingly and uncomfortably. "If a man didn't know her real well, he might easily get the wrong idea just by watching her walk down the street. But she didn't mean anything by it. She was just as innocent as the day is long."

Timothy Rourke shrugged and said, "Some women just can't help it." He drained his glass and pushed back his chair and stood up. "Well, thanks a lot for your informa-tion, Mr. Wilsson. I'll probably be seeing you around."

He walked out, lifting one hand in a wave to the bar-tender as he passed behind the backs of the men seated at the bar, went down the street outside to his car and got in and drove a block where he made a U-Turn and drove back on Main Street, slowing up in front of City Hall which housed the police department, and looking for a parking space.

At that moment he saw Patrolman Leroy Smith coming

down the walk to the street, and he double-parked and leaned out and waved to the young man, and Leroy saw him and hurried to the side of his car and said, "Hi, Mr. Rourke. Something you wanted?"

Rourke unlatched the door and said, "Climb in," waited until he was inside and then pulled ahead slowly. He said, "I've got a little job for you. Where's your finger-printing equipment?"

"I keep it all at home. I've got a little laboratory fixed up there. . . ."

"Which way is home?"

"Just a couple of blocks. Turn to your right at the second corner. Matter of fact, I was going home for a snack. Then I have to go back on duty at headquarters at one. What kind of job, Mr. Rourke?"

Rourke said, "I'll show you when we get there." He turned at the indicated corner and Leroy pointed out a neat stucco house in the middle of the block. "Turn in the driveway and stop. We can go in the side entrance."

The reporter followed him into a small, neat room with a bare porcelain table in the middle of it, a sink with running water, and shelves along one wall holding an array of neatly-labeled jars and bottles.

"I know it doesn't look like very much," Leroy said hesitantly, "but I've got all my reference books here, and all the equipment I've gathered together ever since I studied chemistry in high school. What was it you wanted?"

Rourke pulled the paper sack out of the baggy side pocket of his coat and laid it on the table. He took hold of the end of it with the pint inside and lifted it, and the shot-glass rolled out on the porcelain surface.

"I want you to dust that for fingerprints," he told the young policeman, "and then get your magnifying glass out and we'll compare what you find with the prints you lifted off that highball glass in the Blake house this morning. A person doesn't have to be an expert to make that sort of comparison."

Leroy Smith's jaw drooped incredulously. "Do you mean you've found out who was there last night and had a drink with her?"

"Get out your powder and duster and we'll see. And be sure you keep it damn well under your hat if I turn out to be right," grated Rourke. "Just because a man had a drink with her doesn't mean he strangled her."

11

At three o'clock that afternoon Harry Wilsson's secretary entered the private office at the rear of his insurance agency and informed her employer that a Mr. Shayne was in the outer office and wanted to see him.

The name meant nothing to Wilsson, and he asked somewhat irritably, "Is he selling something?"

Miss Andrews said she didn't think so. "He doesn't *look* like a salesman, and he *said* it's a personal matter of some importance."

Wilsson nodded and said, "All right," and she went out, and he picked up one of the papers scattered on the desk in front of him and was pretending to read it when a tall, wide-shouldered man with rumpled, red hair and cold, gray eyes came quietly through the door and closed it behind him. Wilsson put the paper down and looked at his visitor with a questioning frown. He was certain he had never seen the man before, and he said somewhat brusquely, "Shayne, is it? What can I do for you?"

"Just answer a few questions," Shayne told him, pulling a chair close to the desk and sitting down without waiting for an invitation. "I'm a private investigator from Miami helping your local police on the Blake murder case."

"Oh, you're *that* Shayne? Michael Shayne. Well, I've heard about you, all right. I didn't know Ollie would have the gumption to call someone like you in, but I'm mighty glad he did. Maybe we'll get somewhere now."

Shayne said briskly, "I hope so. Right now I'm gathering a little background, and I understand you may have been the last person to see the victim alive."

"That's possible. My wife and I, that is. Ellie Blake stopped by our house about four o'clock yesterday afternoon."

"And that's the last time you saw her?"

Wilsson nodded. "She stayed fifteen or twenty minutes, I guess."

"Did you notice anything unusual about her, Mr. Wilsson? Was she nervous or upset? Anything at all to indicate that she had any reason to expect anything out of the ordinary to occur last night?"

"I don't think so. I'm not sure I know just what you're getting at."

"I'm wondering," said Shayne blandly, "if she might have had a date for later on in the evening. With some man, perhaps. I understand it was the last night her husband planned to be away from home and that Mrs. Blake was, well . . . ." Shayne spread out his hands and shrugged. "An attractive woman to say the least."

"There wouldn't be anything like that." Wilsson looked properly shocked. "Not with Ellie Blake. No. I think you're barking up the wrong tree there, Mr. Shayne. It was some stranger in town. Some sex maniac."

Shayne said, "You're probably right, and that's going to make it the most difficult sort of case there is. What did you do last evening?"

"Me? Do you mean you want me to give you an alibi?"

"It wouldn't do any harm," Shayne told him cheerfully. "What I would like to do is get a picture of what the people closest to Ellie Blake were doing last night. Every alibi I can clinch eliminates one more possibility. Nothing personal about it. Just tell me where you were."

"Well, let's see. As a matter of fact I drove over to Turner's Junction right after dinner, to try and see a man and sign him up for life insurance. That's about forty miles each way on a back country road. I got home around eleven, I guess. I remember it was just after eleven. Minerva, that's my wife, was sitting up watching the eleven o'clock news, and we went to bed right after it ended."

"Did you sell the policy?"

"As a matter of fact, he wasn't home when I got there," Wilsson said disgustedly. "Jed Turner. He's got a farm the other side of the Junction and I telephoned when I got there. No answer. I was pretty sore after making that long drive out to see him, and I hung around for about an hour and called twice more. Then I gave it up as a bad job and came home. I remember telling Minerva when I got back that *that* was a wasted evening if there ever was one. But that's the way it goes in the insurance business."

"Did you see anyone you know while you were waiting in Turner's Junction?"

"No. It's hardly more than a crossroads. There's a beer joint and poolhall, but I didn't feel like going in. I just sat in my car and smoked. Made my calls from a public telephone booth beside the road."

"Then you actually have no proof you were there last night?"

"Good Lord, man! Do I have to prove where I was? I remember telling Minerva when I left that I was going over to see Jed Turner."

Michael Shayne settled back in his chair and said bleakly, "You're lying, Wilsson."

"Now see here," sputtered the insurance broker. "You can't come in here and start saying. . . ."

"I am in here and I am saying," Shayne interrupted him calmly. "Do you want to talk to me here in the privacy of your own office, or shall we go down to police headquarters? You see, Wilsson, right now my friend Tim Rourke, and I are the only ones who know you dropped in at the Blake house last evening and had a drink with your best friend's wife while he was in Miami. I don't want to pillory any man unnecessarily, but I'm working on a murder case and we'll spread it all over town if you want it that way." His voice was even and cold and utterly un-compromising.

"But you're all wrong." Wilsson stared across the desk at him aghast. "I wasn't near Ellie Blake last night. It's a made-up lie if anybody says different."

"You left your fingerprints on a highball glass sitting in her living room beside the glass she drank out of. The police have those prints on file, but they haven't got around yet to checking them against yours. When they do, everyone in town will know where you were last night."

Harry Wilsson crumpled up in front of his cold gaze and put his hands over his face and moaned softly.

Shayne got out a cigarette and lighted it and smoked thoughtfully. When Wilsson took his hands away from his face it was a sick, gray color and he kept wetting his lips with the tip of his tongue as he poured out his story in a low, hoarse voice that trembled with self-pity.

"I just stopped in for a drink. It was early, just past eight and I saw her light was on as I drove past and I thought I'd just go in and say good night and cheer her up maybe. And that's what I did. We had one little drink in the living room and you can't make anything wrong out of that. How could I know some murdering bastard would break in and kill her after I left?"

Shayne said disbelievingly, "If it was so completely innocent, why didn't you mention it to your wife when you got home? Wouldn't that have been the natural thing to do?"

"Not if you knew Minerva, you'd know it wouldn't.

She's got a nasty mind and she's always been suspicious of Ellie. I never would have heard the last of it, if I'd told her. She'd be forever prying and asking questions. Like: 'Did you kiss her good night? Did she rub up against you?' Nasty things like that. And then she would have told Marv as soon as he got home for sure," he went on bitterly, "and maybe get *him* thinking Ellie and I'd been carrying on behind his back. No, sir, I certainly didn't see any good reason to blab it out to Minerva last night."

"But how about this morning? After you found out what happened in the night. Didn't you realize you had information that should have been given to the police?"

"This morning?" Harry Wilsson gulped and swallowed hard. "God, I didn't know what to do. People might think all kinds of things with Ellie dead like that. You know how it is. And I realized it was going to look funny when I told about driving over to Turner's Junction and hanging around an hour without being able to prove it. Some folks, including Minerva, would be sure to think I'd spent all that time with Ellie."

"And," said Shayne quietly, "I, Mr. Wilsson."

"What? What do you mean by that?"

"Your story does sound fishy, you know. Look. We're both grown up, and we both know the facts of life. Right now, we're talking off the record. I assume you know that a medical examination of Mrs. Blake discloses that some man had intercourse with her at about the time of her death? Possibly slightly before . . . perhaps soon afterward."

"I didn't know that," muttered Wilsson, his face ashen. "Even so, it has nothing to do with me. I guess everybody assumes that she was raped while she was murdered."

"There's one way you can prove it has nothing to do with you," Shayne told him briskly. "What is your blood group?"

"I don't know. What has that to do with it?"

"It is a medical fact," Shayne told him, "that semen, along with most of the other body fluids, such as saliva and perspiration, can be tested for blood-grouping, just as is done with blood itself. If you want to prove you weren't intimate with Mrs. Blake last night, give us a sample of your blood. If yours is a different group, you'll be in the clear."

"But suppose it happens to be the same group?" cried Wilsson in agitation. "That wouldn't prove it came from me. It's like a paternity case. You can prove a man can't be the father . . . but you can't prove he is, just because his blood is the right group."

"That's true," Shayne agreed gravely. "However, there is another test, Wilsson, if you're willing to have it made. Unlike blood, the spermatazoa in the seminal fluid have definite individual characteristics that are much like a man's fingerprints. In other words, under microscopic examination it is possible to ascertain whether a certain sample of sperm originated in you or did not. Do you follow me? If you're willing to give me a sample for comparison. . . ."

"Oh, God," groaned Wilsson. "I didn't know that. I never heard *that* before."

"You know it now," Shayne told him coldly. "Why

don't you break down and tell me the truth about what happened between you and Ellie Blake last night? If you didn't kill her, I assure you I'm not a damn bit interested in what else you did. But I need the truth from you at this point."

"Kill her? Good God! *Me?* Why would I kill her?"

"Women have been known to resist a man's advances," Shayne said bleakly. "And men have been known to strangle a woman to get what they want from her."

"Good God in heaven, that's not the way it was. Not that I want to say Ellie was forward, but she . . . she sure didn't fight me off. Lord, I guess I better tell you the whole thing just the way it was."

"I guess you'd better," said Shayne, "though I make no positive guarantee I'm going to believe you."

"Yeh . . . I . . . Well, it was just one of those things. You know, it had been building up for a long time without either one of us ever actually trying to do anything about it. You can't, in a small town like this. There just isn't any opportunity. And then suddenly last night there was an opportunity. Probably the only one there'd ever be, and both of us realized it. I didn't know when I stopped by her house . . . I didn't know whether anything would happen or not . . . whether she *wanted* anything to happen. But there we were together suddenly, all alone. With Marv due back today and both of us a little tight on account of, I guess, because she'd made the drinks pretty strong and neither one of us is used to drinking much. And so it just happened. I wish to God it hadn't. I'd give a million dollars right now if I hadn't stopped by to see Ellie last night. But I did! And then this morning when I heard what happened . . . My God, Mr. Shayne, how do you think I felt? Like I was sort of to blame, but . . . I don't see how I could be. I swear she was perfectly all right when I left a few minutes before eleven. There wasn't a sign of anything wrong. I was careful not to even turn on my automobile lights while I coasted down away from the house, and there wasn't a soul around and I'm sure nobody saw me. So I don't see what Ellie and I did had to do with what happened to her later, but I've still got that awful feeling inside me that if I *hadn't* done it everything might be different. And I don't know I can stand to face Marv when he comes home. Having Sissy there right in the house is bad enough. And if Minerva ever finds out. . . ."

Shayne said thoughtfully, "You're sure you left a little before eleven?"

"Minerva will tell you that," Wilsson assured him eagerly. "Like I told you before, it was a little after eleven when I got home and she was watching the news on TeeVee. So whatever happened to Ellie must've happened after eleven o'clock."

"If you're telling the truth," said Shayne.

"Well, I am. Like I say, I can prove I was home a few minutes after eleven."

"But you haven't proved that Ellie Blake was still alive when you left her bedroom," Shayne pointed out grimly.

Harry Wilsson stared at him in consternation and horror, his jaw drooping open slackly. "Why would I hurt her?"

e cried out. "My Lord, she'd just . . . well, you know."
He swallowed hard and appeared to be on the verge of
ears. "I don't know what else I can say," he quavered.

"I don't either," Shayne said uncompromisingly. He
looked at his watch and got up. "For the moment I'm going
o keep this confidential, Wilsson. But you're not in the
clear. I'll be talking to you again." He turned and strode out
of the office hurriedly.

12

Marvin Blake awoke that day slowly and unwillingly. He had a terrible, splitting headache and his mouth tasted of dry cow manure (the way he imagined dry cow manure tasted). He was enveloped in a grayish fog of semi-consciousness which he hugged about him gratefully and into which he retreated each time his mind threatened to pierce the barrier into full awareness.

Mercifully, memory was anesthetized for a long period of drugged half-wakefulness during which he fought back against the horror of fully realizing where he was and why he was there.

Slowly, inexorably, consciousness came to him, and with it the horrible phantasms of memory which had been floating, wraithlike, beyond the barrier; which he had sensed, but refused to give credence to.

It came back to him with a sickening, savage onrush of reality and with stark clarity. His body trembled violently and then stiffened, and tears flowed from his eyes, and he knew an awful sense of desolation and of self-pity.

He knew where he was and why he was there. He recalled planning to kill himself last night, and he was filled with bitter self-revulsion for having failed to carry out his plan.

He opened his eyes wide and discovered that he was lying on his back, fully clothed, on top of the spread on a hotel bed. Overhead, an unshaded electric bulb cast a sickly yellow light over the bare room with its drawn shade and tightly closed window. Beyond the faded shade, bright sunlight told him it was well into the next day, but he had not the faintest idea what time it was.

He had passed out, of course, he realized bitterly and with self-loathing. He was a weakling who had sought strength from a whiskey bottle to bolster up his resolution and had, instead, brought himself to this miserable state where time must go on and the galling future must be faced.

He closed his eyes tightly for a long moment, and then gritted his teeth and forced himself to turn on his side so he could see his wristwatch.

It was almost two-thirty. In the afternoon. The train from Miami was due to come through about three o'clock! The same train that he had happily planned to come home on when he departed for the convention a few days ago.

He was expected on that train. Sissy would be at the station to greet him and throw her sweet arms about his neck and press her face against him. Oh, God. Sissy!

With sudden sure clarity he knew it was Sissy who mattered now. He mustn't fail Sissy. Her mother and Harry Wilsson!

He forced the memory to the back of his mind at the same time as he forced his rebellious body to sit up in bed and his legs to swing over the side.

A flooding wave of nausea engulfed him and he bent forward retching, and then vomited on the floor between his wide-spread feet. Some of the vomit splashed up onto to his shoes, and he stared at the stains dully and reminded himself that he must wash them off before Sissy saw them.

Because Sissy must never know. She must never suspect. He *did* have something to live for. He was grateful, now, that God had intervened last night and caused him to take that second drink from the bottle before he took his own life.

His senses were spinning and his head was splitting wide open as he shambled to his feet and made his way unsteadily into the bathroom. The physical effort caused him to vomit again, and he hung laxly over the toilet seat, trembling and white-faced, retching again and again until it seemed that his very guts would be wrenched loose and would have to come up.

And suddenly he felt better. He was still weak and shaking, but the sharp, screaming pain in his head had subsided to a dull, endurable ache.

He loosened his collar and removed his tie, and ran cold water in the basin and soaked a hand-towel in it to slosh over his face and neck. He found a glass in the cabinet above the lavatory and washed the taste of dry manure out of his mouth and drank two glassfuls of the wonderful stuff, and then dried his face and consulted his watch again.

Miraculously, less than ten minutes had passed since he had looked at it before. He went back into the bedroom and grimaced when he saw the whiskey bottle on the bureau, less than half full now, and the water glass sitting beside it. His suitcase stood at the foot of the bed, opened, and he knelt down and groped for his razor. He started to search for fresh blades, and then he remembered clearly. The new packet he had taken out the night before still lay unopened on the bed.

And on the rug lay the pad of yellow paper with lined pages. He stared down at the words: *"To whom it may concern"* and underneath that, the scrawled, "I, Marvin Blake, wish to state. . . ." That was as far as he'd got last night. And now he was glad that was as far as he'd got. Now, when he got off the train at Sunray there must be nothing to indicate that he had not spent the night in Miami as previously planned. He must be shaved and look reasonably neat. A hangover didn't matter. It would be accepted as a natural result of cutting loose at the last night of the convention. There was no reason in the world for anyone to suspect anything else, he told himself. No one had actually seen him leave the hotel yesterday afternoon. None of the fellows would really have missed him last night . . . not enough to make any queries, certainly. He doubted whether any of the other delegates would have been taking the train today. Practically all of them had driven their cars to the city. After all, it was an auto dealers' convention, and he remembered that Harry had kidded him about taking the train instead of driving his own car.

Harry!

Oh, God. Harry. Would he ever again in the future be able to think of that name without a sudden tightening of his heart, an awful sinking sensation in the pit of his stomach, a traumatic trembling.

He hurried into the bathroom and shaved himself sketchily. Then he forced himself to take time to comb his hair carefully, replace his tie, and scrub the vomit off his shoes with the wet hand-towel.

He left the whiskey bottle sitting just as it was on the bureau, replaced his razor and closed his bag, and still had fifteen minutes until train-time when he went out of the hotel room and locked the door behind him.

Downstairs, he found a pimply-faced young man at the desk in place of the rheumy-eyed old man who had checked him in last night, and he slid his room-key across with a ten-dollar bill, muttering, "I'm checking out," and averted his face while the young man yawned and checked his registration and languidly counted out his change.

Outside the hotel was bright, hot sunlight, and Marvin Blake sweated from every pore of his body as he walked toward the railroad station carrying his heavy bag. He felt faint, and he thought surely he would have to stop and set the bag down and be sick right there in public on the sidewalk, but somehow he managed to keep moving along at a steady pace, and he reached the station five minutes before the train was due, but he went straight on to the platform to board it without buying a ticket to Sunray from the office inside.

It would be smarter and safer, he thought, to pay cash for a ticket to the conductor on the train. Then there wouldn't be any record made of the transaction, and no chance that the local stationmaster would remember having sold a ticket between the two towns if the question ever arose.

Not that there was any chance it would ever arise, Marvin assured himself while the train from Miami thundered in and he waited for one of the coaches to stop in front of him so he could get aboard. No one in the world, he thought, had any reason to suspect he hadn't stayed for the final night of the convention in Miami last night as he had planned.

No one in the whole world would ever know that he had been in Sunray Beach last night and what had happened there. If only it hadn't ever happened, he thought desperately as he settled himself into an empty coach seat and waited for the train to hurry. If only it were possible to turn back the clock, efface last night and its horror.

He settled himself down on the seat and tried to make himself feel as though none of it *had* happened, as though he were just plain Marvin Blake returning from the convention and looking forward eagerly to greeting his wife and his child when he got off the train at Sunray.

Because that's the way he should be feeling, he told himself. That's the way he had to act when he got off the train. As though nothing had happened. As though last night had not been.

The conductor came through and uninterestedly accepted his cash fare for the short run to Sunray Beach, and passed on forward through the train, and Marvin closed his eyes and wished his head would stop aching and tried to pretend that everything was just the way it had always been, and the clacking of the wheels almost put him to sleep for a moment, and it all began to seem like a dream, and suddenly he was uneasily aware of a sort of pressure against his chest, and he put his hand up there, half in a dream-state, and he felt that hard lump of the gift box in his breast pocket containing the pretty earrings he had bought as a gift for Ellie in Miami, and a fierce anger took possession of him and he took the box out of his pocket and glared at it.

He ought to throw it away, he thought. He ought to destroy it. What an utter damned fool he had been! To give up his last night in Miami to save enough money to afford the earrings to take home to a bitch of a wife who was already planning to spend the evening in the arms of his best friend.

Tears came into his eyes again, but he blinked them away angrily and put the square gift box back in his pocket. He'd better hang onto it, he thought. It would look better that way. Him bringing a special present home to Ellie, all wrapped up and with a card in it. It would go to show how much he loved Ellie and trusted her.

That was very important, now. Much more important than it had ever been in the past when he *had* loved and trusted her, and never had any reason to be otherwise. He couldn't say why it was more important now. Obscurely, though, he knew it was on account of Sissy. Sissy must never know. She must never be allowed to guess. Nothing else was important from this time onward in life. He must

keep that always in mind. He must guard every word hence-
forth, every inflection.

Marvin Blake's heart pounded and his hands were clammy
as the afternoon train lunged on down the tracks closer and
closer to home.

Who would be at the station to meet him? How would
he carry it off? Suppose Harry Wilsson were to be there?
He and Minerva. It would be the most natural thing in the
world, they being his and Ellie's closest friends. But would
Harry have the guts to face him after last night?

How *could* a man do that? Of course, Harry didn't have
an inkling that Marvin knew. He'd probably be afraid *not*
to come to the station to meet his train, Marvin decided
contemptuously after a bit of thought. It would be like
Harry to brazen it out. Hell, maybe he had been brazening
it out for a long time and was used to it. Maybe last night
hadn't been the first time for him and Ellie . . . not by a
long shot.

The conductor came walking back through the train,
and he called out, "Sunray Beach," while he was passing
Marvin's seat.

The train swayed a little as it began slowing down for
the station, and Marvin got up and pushed his suitcase out
into the aisle with his foot, and braced himself for a moment, leaning down to try and peer out the window as they
ground into the station, but he couldn't see anything in
the bright sunlight outside the grimy window, and he
straightened up and got a firm grip on his bag and walked
back to the exit where he was the only passenger to get off.

He stood at the bottom of the steps for a moment on the

narrow cindered strip, blinking his eyes and looking up and down the track for a familiar face.

He saw three men walking toward him unhurriedly from the direction of the station. He recognized only one of them, Chief of Police Ollie Jenson. The other two were strangers.

He looked beyond them to the station platform, but saw no one else who appeared to be there to meet him. Not even Harry Wilsson.

Marvin Blake shifted his suitcase from his right hand to his left, and advanced to meet the three men.

13

Chief Jenson stepped forward in front of the two strangers and extended his hand, exclaiming effusively, "Hello there, Marv old boy. Had yourself quite a time in the city, I reckon. You look like you hung one on last night for sure." He gripped Marvin's right hand tightly and shook it with more enthusiasm than seemed necessary under the circumstances, and Marvin smiled with an obvious effort and admitted, "I have got a hangover, Ollie. Where is everybody? I thought sure. . . ."

"Well, I got a couple fellows here I want you to meet, Marv. Come up from Miami special to see you. Mr. Timothy Rourke. He's a reporter on the Miami *News*, Marv. And Mr. Michael Shayne. Meet Marvin Blake, gentlemen."

Marvin looked confused and somewhat frightened as he allowed his limp hand to be shaken by both men, and he muttered, "From Miami? I just came from there. I don't see. . . ."

"Tell you what, Marv. It's like a newspaper interview, see?" said Ollie Jenson, stooping to pick up Blake's suitcase and taking him firmly by the elbow. "My car's parked right here in the shade. Let's all go over and sit down comfortable, huh?"

"Wait a minute now, Ollie." Marvin resisted the pressure on his elbow and looked toward the station again. "Where's Ellie and Sissy? I made sure they'd be down to meet the train. What's going on here anyway? Has something happened that you're keeping back from me?" His voice rose shrilly, underlaid with panic.

"Now Marv, boy, you just take it easy," Jenson counseled him with an appealing glance at Rourke and Shayne for assistance. "Don't you worry about them. You'll be seeing Sissy all right in just a few minutes. Let's just get this little business took care of first, then I'll drive you straight on home."

He dropped his hand from Marvin's arm as Shayne and Rourke moved up on either side of the man, and he moved on a few paces ahead of the trio toward his police sedan which waited nearby at the end of the station parking lot.

"Just a few questions, Mr. Blake," Timothy Rourke said quietly. "First off, where were you last night?"

"Where do you suppose I was?" snapped Marvin. "At the tail-end of the convention getting drunk and making a fool of myself . . . that's what. Why is the Miami *News* interested in that? I don't get this at all. There's something wrong, isn't there? By God, if you don't tell me. . . ."

"We want *you* to tell *us*, Blake," Shayne interrupted him.

"We know you weren't at the Atlantic Palms Hotel last night. You checked out at four o'clock yesterday afternoon."

"So you know that, do you?" demanded Marvin Blake bitterly. "What's it to you what I did last night? Can't a man have any privacy? Who are you, anyhow, to be asking questions?" He doggedly stopped in his tracks and looked the big redhead up and down with challenging eyes. "I don't think I got your name."

"Mike Shayne," the detective told him.

"What paper do *you* work for? What is this anyhow?"

"We're asking the questions, Blake," Shayne told him evenly. "Any reason why you don't want to tell us where you spent last night?"

"Can you give me any good reason why I should?" Marvin faced the two of them defiantly, and then suddenly turned and hurried away from them toward Jenson who was putting his suitcase in the back seat of the sedan.

"You got to tell me, Ollie," he jerked out desperately. "We're friends, aren't we? What is this all about? Something's happened, hasn't it? A minute ago you said I'd see *Sissy* in just a minute. What about Ellie? You didn't mention her. What about my wife? Has something happened to Ellie? You got to tell me. I've got a right to know."

"Well now, Marv. . . ." Jenson looked past the distraught auto dealer at the two men from Miami for a signal. Shayne shrugged wide shoulders and nodded.

"I'm sorry, Marv." The police chief put a fleshy hand on Blake's shoulder and squeezed it tightly. "I hate to have to tell you like this. Dag-nab it, yes. Something bad has happened to Ellie. She got herself murdered last night, Marv."

"Murdered? Ellie?" Marvin shrank back from him, aghast. "I don't believe it, Ollie. I just don't believe it. Not *Ellie.*" He began to shake violently, staring at the chief as though hoping for some reprieve, but seeing none in Jenson's unhappy countenance.

Shayne stepped up beside him briskly and said, "It's a hell of a thing to hit a man with, Blake. I've been in this business a lot of years and I never have found a good way to break it to a husband."

"Shayne?" Marvin Blake said dully, staring at him as though seeing him for the first time. "Michael Shayne. I know. You're a detective, aren't you? Then it must be true." His voice broke and he turned back to Jenson. "What about Sissy? Goddam your soul to hell, Ollie. *Tell me the truth.* Is Sissy . . . ?"

"Sissy's all *right,*" Jenson told him. "She's waiting for you right now at the Wilsson house where Minerva's looking after her, and you got to get hold of yourself and keep your chin up when you go to see her. She's a right brave little girl, Sissy is, and she needs her daddy right now more'n she ever needed him in her life before."

"Sissy," Marvin cried out in pain. "I've got to go to her. What are we waiting here for? Goddam it, Ollie. . . ."

"Now you just take it easy, Marv. You'll see Sissy soon enough. Let's us get a few things straight first, and then we won't have to bother you later on."

"Who did it? How did it *happen?*" demanded Marvin exactly as though Jenson had not spoken.

Jenson swallowed hard and looked appealingly at the Miami detective. Shayne said evenly, "Your wife was strangled to death in her own bed, Blake. Chief Jenson suspects some transient who may have got into the house through the front window. You're just holding up our investigation by refusing to tell us where you were last night. I'm sorry to have to say this, but you may as well understand that a woman's husband is always the first suspect in a case like this. The sooner we can mark you off the better."

"*Me?* You suspect me?" demanded Marvin incredulously. "You think I . . . I'd do that to Ellie? I loved her." He swayed back against the car and began sobbing helplessly. "My God, you fool, I loved her. Don't you understand that? She was my *wife* . . . Sissy's mother!"

"So where were you last night?" Shayne's even voice beat at him through his hysteria.

"Well, I wasn't out here murdering anybody, that's for sure. My God, Ollie! You don't believe that for a minute. Why don't you tell him? I got a right to go home."

"Well, now, Marv," Jenson said uncomfortably. "It's like Mr. Shayne says. Sooner we get that cleared up, sooner we can get onto finding the man that really did it. All you got to do is tell us, Marv. Just don't try to lie at a time like this. We know you checked out of the hotel. So, where'd you go and where'd you stay last night? That's all you got to tell us. There's just the three of us men-folks here, Marv," he went on earnestly. "It won't have to go no further than here. We don't care a damn if you shacked up with some fancy woman, or what."

Marvin Blake wilted back against the car and hung his head. "So that's what you think? You think I was out whoring around while Ellie was getting murdered?"

"It wasn't like you knew it was going to happen to her," Jenson consoled him. "None of us'll fault you on that. You just come on and tell us, Marv. I'll tell you one thing right now," he hurried on. "Not another soul in town knows you *wasn't* at the convention last night where you was supposed to be. No need anybody ever should know, I reckon, including Sissy, if you'll just tell us the truth so's we can check it out. No matter for you to be ashamed, no matter what you did."

"Ashamed? Oh, my God." Marvin Blake put both hands over his face and it was difficult to tell whether he was laughing or crying. Watching his shaking shoulders there in the hot sunlight, and listening to him, Shayne thought it was about a fifty-fifty mixture of laughter and tears, both of them wavering on the verge of hysteria.

The three men waited uncomfortably, grouped closely around him, until the seizure slowly subsided. He took his hands away from his face and lifted his head, blinking and licking his lips. "It's funny . . . almost," he said hoarsely. "What you think. When I . . . all I wanted was to get away from that hotel and the convention last night and get home to my wife . . . and not get pissy-assed drunk the way I knew I'd do if I stayed on there with the other boys. If I just had of done it," he moaned, his face twitching with the horror of it. "If I just had made it like I planned . . . Ellie might be all *right*. I'd of been here, don't you see? Nothing like that could have happened, if I'd just been here. It's my fault, don't you see? Because I took that first drink like a damn fool, and then another one and another. And so I ended up drunker than maybe I would have if I *had* stayed on at the hotel, and I didn't even make it home like I planned to do."

"Tell us about it," said Shayne gently. "Just the straight

facts. Don't blame yourself. You can see it would have happened just the same if you'd stayed over as you meant to."

"Well, I . . . it just came to me suddenly yesterday that I didn't *want* to stay on for the big doings last night, but that I'd rather come on back home. And it seemed silly to waste all that money spending an extra night at the hotel and the dinner and drinks and all, and so I just decided to slip out without saying anything to anybody, to avoid any arguments, you know. Because the others would laugh at me and make jokes and say dirty things about how I just couldn't stand to be away from my wife for another night . . . and I didn't see how it was anybody's business what I did." He looked about defiantly at the three men in front of him.

"Check-out time at the hotel was four o'clock, even if there wasn't any train back to Sunray until after six, but I could save a whole night's room-rent by checking out then, and so I did."

"You mean the ten-twenty express from Miami, Marv?" Jenson broke in with a frown. "It don't even stop here."

"Yes, it does. To let off passengers, if there are any. It says so right on the time-table. I looked it up there in my hotel room, and then was when I decided. One of the reasons I decided," he went on in a suddenly hushed voice, "was because there was the prettiest pair of earrings in a little store next to the hotel that I wanted to buy for Ellie for a present, but they cost twenty-eight dollars and I didn't feel like I could afford it. But I figured I'd save at least that much by skipping last night and coming straight home, and so I went into the store and bought them."

He raised his right hand slowly and hesitantly to his breast pocket and drew out the gaily wrapped box. "They're right here." His face worked convulsively and he paused to swallow twice before he could go on. "She'll never see them now," he half-whispered. "She'll never know." He blinked back tears and smiled entreatingly at them. "I just can't believe it. Not yet I can't. They were just *right* for her. The earrings, I mean. I just couldn't wait to see her face when I came home and surprised her and she opened up the box." He paused, looking down at the box and turning it over and over in his hands.

Chief Ollie Jenson cleared his throat loudly. "Well, now, Marv, what I say is none of us know for sure. What a body knows or doesn't know after . . . well, what I mean is, it don't do any good to think about that now. It's the intention that counted."

"Maybe . . . Sissy will like them when she grows up," said Marvin unsteadily and somewhat vaguely. He sighed and put the earrings back into his pocket. "Where was I?"

"You'd just checked out of the hotel and bought those earrings to bring home to Ellie on the ten-twenty Express," Jenson reminded him.

"That's right. Well, I walked on down toward the station carrying my suitcase. I had plenty of time and didn't want to waste any money on a taxicab. And I thought I'd better get a bite to eat because even if there was a diner on the train they charge like the dickens for even a sandwich and a cup of coffee.

"So I stopped at a place about a block from the station and went in and set my bag down to rest and get a bite to eat. And I still had almost two hours before the train, so I thought I'd have a highball first before I ate. And it tasted real good, and I was sort of celebrating because I was feeling so good about coming home ahead of time and surprising Ellie and all . . . and so I had another one, and I guess maybe another, and then it was getting on toward train time and I'd already spent as much on the drinks as I'd planned to pay for a whole supper, and so I decided I just as well have one more drink and skip the food altogether."

He shook his head and looked shame-faced at the recollection. "It was a cock-eyed, dam-fool thing to do. I'm not used to drinking much, and I guess they hit me . . . without any supper and all. I just sort of vaguely remember getting out of there and going on to the station in time to board the train before it pulled out, and I got a seat in the smoker, and I remember putting my return ticket up in the little metal clip on the back of the seat in front of me where the conductor would see it when he came through, and then the train started out and I dozed off.

"I was pretty sleepy, you see," he added by way of a weak explanation. "Being up all hours at the convention every night when I'm used to getting to bed at ten o'clock at home at the latest. That and the whiskey I'd drunk. So I guess I slept straight through until I woke up suddenly thinking I'd heard somebody call Sunray Beach.

"And there we were stopped at a station and I looked out a window and it looked like the Sunray station, and I heard somebody yelling 'All aboard' outside, and I jumped up and grabbed my suitcase and ran back to the door and got off the steps just as the train pulled out.

"And there I stood." He looked at them blank-faced, seemingly reliving the appalling moment of realization that had come to him. "I saw right away it wasn't Sunray," he explained. "It was Moonray Beach instead. The first big town south of here," he explained to Rourke and Shayne. "About thirty miles down the road. I felt like the biggest kind of fool there is. Standing there in the middle of the night and not another train until this one today. And the liquor I had drunk was dying inside me and I had a head-ache, and I was just plumb disgusted with myself and every-thing. I never did feel like such a fool in my life before. And I decided right then and there that the best thing for me to do was spend the night and just catch this train on up here today and say nothing about it to anybody, and so that's what I did.

"There was a restaurant still open down the street from the station and I walked down there and had a couple of drinks and then got a sandwich, and then I went on up to a hotel that's only a couple of blocks away and got a room for the night."

"Haven't you listened to a radio or talked with anybody all morning?" asked Ollie Jenson incredulously. "I'd think Moonray Beach would be plumb full and bubbling over with a murder right up the road here. Seems mighty funny you didn't know anything about what happened to Ellie when it went out over the radio at seven o'clock this morn-ing and has been on all the newscasts ever since I guess."

Marvin hesitated as though trying to make up his mind about something, then shrugged and shook his head. "Tell you the truth, I slept right straight through until just before time to catch the train on up here. Didn't talk to anybody or hear any news on the radio."

"From ten-thirty or eleven o'clock last night until three o'clock this afternoon?" Jenson said disbelievingly. "That's a mighty long time to sleep straight through in a hotel room, Marv. I hope to God you can prove that's what you did. Don't you agree with me, Mr. Shayne?" he asked importantly.

The redhead nodded. "I'd like to have the name of the hotel . . . and the restaurant where you went after getting off the train."

Marvin rubbed his hand tiredly across his eyes. "It's the Elite Hotel. Right on Main Street. I don't know about the restaurant, but it's right down the street. Oh, hell," he added miserably, "if you do any checking up you'll find out anyhow, so I might as well admit it. Just to finish off being a complete damn fool last night, when I finally got to the hotel the liquor I'd drunk in Miami was still churning up inside me and I didn't feel like I'd ever get to sleep. So I asked the desk clerk if he had a bottle he'd sell me, and he did have one with only a couple of drinks gone from it. So I took that up to my room and poured out about a waterglass full and drank it off straight, and *that* finished me up, I can tell you. I passed right out cold on the bed and didn't move a finger until two-thirty this afternoon. Then I went straight to the station and got on the train and came home, and here I am. Now it's time *you* did some talking, Ollie. I think I got a right to go see Sissy now."

Jenson glanced at Shayne, who nodded and said, "I think so, too, Chief. I'll just check his story as a formality, but I think you'd better go on looking for your transient killer."

14

Alonzo Peters lived alone in a decrepit three-room shack in a creek bottom about ten miles inland from Sunray Beach on a winding dirt road that eventually came out on the other end on State Highway 419. It was a desolate stretch of low, hummocky country, covered mostly with scrub palmetto, that resisted cultivation and yielded little to man's best efforts to wrest a living from it.

Alonzo Peters had given up making much of an effort many years ago. He did a little fishing in the creek, a little trapping and hunting in and out of season, and he had a couple of acres of cleared-off land where he grew some straggly vegetables when he was of a mind to plant and cultivate them.

He was a short, stubby-bodied man, with thin, sandy hair, a slack, loose-lipped mouth, and watery blue eyes that were set too close together beneath a low forehead.

He didn't bathe very often and you could tell it by the smell of him on a hot day, and folks circled around him and just tolerated him when he came into Sunray on Saturdays to shop for a few groceries and maybe try to cadge a drink or two at Dave's Bar on Main Street.

He had been born sixth in a family of thirteen sharecroppers' children, and five of the litter had succumbed to pellagra and malnutrition and just dry rot before they reached adolescence. Life had not, in fact, offered many opportunities to Alonzo Peters, and he hadn't done too well with those few that had been offered him. He had squeezed through four years of grade school before he quit and went out into the fields to try and do a day's work and earn a day's wages, but by the time he was sixteen he had come to the conclusion that no man ever got very far ahead in life by hard work, and so he had quit trying and just let himself drift.

Despite his unprepossessing background and physical appearance, Alonzo had managed to marry twice (or maybe just once, people weren't quite sure about that). At least, he'd had two women who came to live with him, and he hadn't had any better luck with them than with most other things he attempted.

Both of them were mail-order wives. He got them out of a correspondence club catalog, and both came from far away in answer to letters he painstakingly wrote to them. The first from up north, and the second from Kentucky.

The first was about fifteen years ago. She was a big moon-faced and broad-beamed widow-woman, and it was rumored around admiringly that she had brought some little dowry with her. Five hundred dollars in cash, a lot of people said; and some put it higher than that. Alonzo had cleaned himself up for the occasion, all shaved and with a haircut and new shiny shoes, and he'd tightened up most of the rattles in his old Ford when he drove into Sunray to meet her at the train.

People had reckoned it was a fine thing for Alonzo Peters. There was a woman, they figured, who'd take him in hand and make something out of him, if any female could.

And she started right in, too, soon as he got her home to that three-room shack in the creek bottom. There were stories around about how she turned the place inside out and scrubbed the floors and walls and even the ceilings with lye soap, and in no time at all there was a small but neat vegetable garden in the back yard, and half a dozen laying chickens and a rooster, and even a Jersey milk cow that he bought from a neighbor for thirty-two dollars in cash. And Alonzo stayed cleaned up pretty well and shaved two or three times a week, and they said she wouldn't permit him to chew tobacco inside the house.

But it just didn't work out somehow. Folks didn't know exactly what happened because they weren't much for visiting back and forth, and to tell the truth she wasn't very friendly towards those who did drop by, she being a Yankee and all, and inclined to look down her nose at them.

Anyhow, Alonzo began to smell again on hot days, and he stopped shaving more than every week or so, and he let it be known finally that she'd just taken off and left him to go back up north. No one saw her go, and he was vague about when and how she'd gone, but they reckoned it wasn't any of their business to pry into the private affairs of a man and his wife, so nobody pestered him with questions.

And after a year or so, he let it get out that she had divorced him, but nobody ever did see the papers and that's why there was some talk around about the rights and the wrongs of it when Alonzo snagged another mail-order woman from Kentucky and went up to Delray to meet her off the train and got married to her at the Justice of the Peace there half an hour after she arrived.

But nobody made much of a fuss as to whether it was a legal marriage or not, because this one did seem right for Alonzo; she was a real country-bred woman from the hill-country, and didn't put on any airs like wearing shoes around the house, and she chewed her own snoose to keep him company with his Mail Pouch.

But Alonzo just wasn't cut out for luck. Six or eight months later she got bit by a water moccasin down by the creek when she was fishing for suckers one day, and she died on him before he got her into town for treatment.

There were some who said he was mighty lazy and slack about getting her into town, it being the second day after she was bit that she died, but others argued just as strongly that it wasn't 'Lonzo's fault because lots of folks got moccasin-bit and you just sucked out the place and slapped a wad of fresh-chewed tobacco on it and the swelling went away and it got all right after a few days.

Anyhow, that was years ago and it looked like Alonzo had given up the idea of having a woman live with him.

He made out all right all alone at his shack, going into town maybe once or twice a week to do a half day's work, trimming up a hedge or pulling weeds for some of the city folks to get cash money for groceries and his Mail Pouch, and a bottle of shine that he bought off Pristine Gaylord who had a little one-gallon still at his place about two miles up the road from Alonzo.

He had a new car, too, to replace the old rattletrap Ford that he'd kept stuck together with baling wire and spit for fifteen or twenty years. Well, not a new one, but a 1952 Chevy that he'd traded for at the Ford Agency in Sunray, getting a fifteen-dollar trade-in allowance for his old car and signing a paper to pay ten dollars a month for twenty-four months for the Chevvy.

Some folks had thought Marvin Blake was a fool to trust Alonzo to pay ten dollars every month, but that was before it got around that Alonzo was paying off the debt by working two hours every week at the Blake house, mowing the lawn and cleaning up around the yard.

That had been going on for two months now, and both Marvin Blake and Alonzo were perfectly satisfied with the arrangement.

And that's why Alonzo was so plumb upset and practically sick to his stomach when he heard the first news about Ellie Blake over the radio at seven o'clock that morning.

She was a mighty fine woman. Always had a smile and a pleasant word for him when she happened to come out the back door when he was working in the yard. And just last week she'd brought him out a can of cold beer and stood and talked to him just as friendly-like while he drank it. And a little breeze had blown up when she turned around and walked back to the kitchen door and he couldn't help noticing the way it tugged at her light cotton dress and pulled it tight against her butt like she didn't have on nary a thing underneath the dress. It reminded him of his first wife. The way she had walked with the wind blowing her dress right after they were first married.

Now the radio said she was dead. Strangled in her own bed at night while her husband was away from home and her all alone there with only her little girl. It was enough to make a man puke just to think about it.

Alonzo sat hunched over his radio and listened avidly to every tiny detail. There weren't many on that first broadcast. Just a recital of the bare facts. They thought it was some hobo. And that he'd maybe got into the house to rob it through that front window that was generally open at the bottom to let a breeze in. They didn't say whether she was raped or not. They didn't say whether she had her clothes on or off when they found her.

Alonzo Peters' pale blue eyes gleamed wetly as he visualized the scene in her upstairs bedroom. They didn't have to say she was naked. That's the way he saw her in his mind's eye. Laying there, humped up on the bed, well-fleshed thighs and buttocks gleaming like ivory in the moonlight.

Was there a moon last night? Yes, there was. More than half full. He remembered how it lay softly on the town when he drove through just before midnight. His heart thudded and he thought back in fright to remember if anyone had seen him, if anyone could place him in Sunray last night.

Suppose they did? Suppose they remembered how he'd been working around the Blake yard recently. Had anyone noticed the way she smiled at him, twitched that butt at him? Did anyone know she had brought him that can of beer last week? If people got to thinking about that . . . and talking!

But, shucks, there wasn't a soul in the world knew he'd passed through Sunray last night on his way home from Delta up the coast. There was a back road from Delta that cut off Sunray and saved a couple of miles coming home. He'd say he took that if anybody asked and no one would know he'd driven down the highway instead. Not a light in the whole town that he'd seen. There wasn't nothing to worry about. They were looking for some bum. Some stranger. The radio said so.

He stayed inside the house all day, close to the radio, twisting the dial for other nearby stations and listening avidly for more details on each succeeding newscast. There weren't many. Just a rehash of the few known facts. They did say delicately that Ellie Blake had been sexually molested, and it was theorized that the crime had been committed by a sexual maniac. The mere suggestion made him angry.

Hell, a man didn't have to be a sexual maniac to want a piece like Ellie Blake had been. The way she shook that thing in a man's face! Tempting him. The way she had tempted him in her backyard that other afternoon. You couldn't tell him she didn't know the effect she had on a man, and that she enjoyed doing it. A teaser. That's what she was. He'd heard that kind of dirty talk about her around town in the past. In a way she had just been asking for what happened to her.

It was on the four o'clock newscast when he heard the startling announcement that the Miami *News* had offered a thousand-dollar cash reward for any information leading to the arrest and conviction of Ellie Blake's murderer. It seemed like they had their star reporter in Sunray covering the case, and they'd hired a high-priced private detective from Miami to come up and look for clues.

Alonzo snorted at this. What could a private detective find? Didn't the radio say there weren't any clues? Just somebody passing through town . . . probably already hundreds of miles away by this time?

But, a thousand-dollar reward. Good God'l'mighty! That was a lot of money. He tried to visualize a thousand dollars and couldn't. About the most cash he'd ever seen in his life at one time was fifty-sixty dollars, he guessed.

Great day in the morning! What a man could do with a whole thousand dollars in cash. Not much a man *couldn't* do with that much money in his pocket. Go to Jacksonville to a high-class hotel and order drinks brought right up to the room, and women, too. Lordy, a man could really have himself a time with a fistful of money like that.

That'd stir things up in Sunray, all right. Plenty of people would sure like to earn that sort of reward. Everybody'd be studying how to get their hands on it. Any nasty little suspicion that anybody had would become important.

It'd start people talking and thinking, all right. If anybody had seen him last night and got to wondering about it . . . anybody on the highway happened to notice his license number late at night!

But, shucks. Who on the highway would notice a man's license number? And he hadn't met anybody after he turned off on the dirt road to home. He was plumb sure he hadn't.

Now, if *he'd* just noticed something he could tell them for the reward. He began studying about it hard. But there wasn't a thing he could think of. If he only could! He could just see himself going in to Chief Ollie Jenson's office and saying importantly, "I guess I'll take that reward, Chief. I just happened to be driving through town about midnight last night . . . on my way home from Delta . . . and I didn't think anything about it at the time, not knowing nothing, of course, about Miz Blake then, but I saw. . . ."

Well, what *had* he seen? What *might* he have seen that would earn him that reward money? He racked his brains and he couldn't think of anything at all that sounded the least bit reasonable.

He turned off the radio when the newscast was ended, and got up from his chair. What he needed was a drink of Pristine's corn.

He went out into the littered side-yard in the hot, late afternoon sunlight and got into his Chevvy, and it made him think of Ellie and Marvin Blake.

He sure felt sorry for that Mr. Blake. He was a right nice fellow for a thing like that to happen to. The radio had told how he had come back on the train from Miami expecting his wife and little girl to meet him at the station. She was a right sweet little girl, that Sissy. Her mama hadn't allowed her to come out and play in the yard with him when he worked there, and that had irked him some, but he had tried not to be mad at Ellie for that. Mothers were always worrying about keeping their little girls fresh and clean-looking and dressed up.

He drove up the rutted road with the Chevvy taking the bumps and holes so smooth you hardly noticed them, and turned off after about two miles on a narrower track that led down toward the creek and a one-room weathered shanty nestled in a grove of scrub pine. The yard was neat and clean in contrast to his own place, and a hound dog stretched lazily in the shade of one of the trees, and Pristine Gaylord came out onto the porch with a wide smile of welcome on his black face when Alonzo shut off the motor.

The name of Gaylord had come down with the family from slave days, and the boy had been named Pristine by his mother at birth because her white folks where she did washing were well-educated and she had heard the word used to indicate something new and bright and shining. Well, she allowed her new baby was just about the newest and brightest and shiningest thing there ever was, and she was probably right at the time, but unfortunately he had grown up into a hulking, ape-like sort of man with a big torso that was much too heavy for his spindly legs, and with a broad, flat face that looked forbidding until he smiled.

Pristine was considered simple-minded by those who knew him, although not quite "teched in the head." It was said about him that he did not know his own strength, and he had spent two long stretches on the chain gang for having badly smashed up opponents of his own race during Saturday free-for-alls when the moonshine had flowed too freely.

Since his latest release, two years previously, Pristine had lived alone in the little shack by the creek, living a happily solitary life and doing whatever drinking he did in the company of his hound dog who was named Franklin D. Roosevelt. He made a little shine and sold it mostly to those who came to his door with a dollar bill to exchange for a quart Mason jar of the white stuff, and he led a quietly uneventful life as behooved a circumspect colored boy who had twice been in trouble with the law.

Now he leaned lazily against a post holding up the porch roof and grinned widely and said in his soft voice, "Good evenin', Mist Peters, suh. Shoah is hot, ain't it?"

Alonzo said, "It sure enough is at that." He got out of his car and slammed the door shut. "You been listening to the radio, Pris?"

"No, suh. I ain't. I bin down to thuh crik mos' all the day runnin' off a li'l batch." He came down off the porch, moving lightly for his hulk, and moved toward a wooden bench in the shade of the trees which caught any vagrant breeze that might be around.

"Then you ain't heard about Ellie Blake up in Sunray last night?" said Alonzo eagerly, following him. "She got herself killed in bed, that's what."

"Do tell? Miz Marvin Blake, I reckon you mean."

"You know the one I mean." Alonzo chuckled obscenely.

"Don't tell me you ain't looked at her walkin' down the street the way she was always doing."

"Nuh-*uh*, Mist Peters. This here colored boy don't never look at no white women the way you mean. I got troubles enough 'thout that. They know who done it to her?"

"Not yet." Alonzo sat on the bench and spat a stream of tobacco juice into the dust between his feet. "They got detectives from Miami and the State Police and all. I reckon they'll be around here to your house any time, checkin' alibis and all. You got one for last night, Pris?"

"Got one what?" The Negro appeared honestly bewildered.

"An alibi. Can you prove where you was at?"

"I was right here to home asleep."

"Can you prove it?"

"Must I needs to?" Pristine wrinkled his forehead. "I ain't bin off the place for three days, an' that's the truf. My ol' pick-up is busted down an' I cain't even get to town to take in a load to my customers what I promised a delivery yestidy."

Alonzo said, "Is that a fact? I reckon that's about all the alibi you need, Pris. How about fetchin' me a quart?"

"Shuah. I get it from back the shed."

Pristine Gaylord got up from his end of the bench and strode toward a shed at the rear of the shack which housed his pick-up truck. Alonzo watched him go, and began to shake violently. "A thousand dollars!" he thought, awed. "A thousand goddamn *dollars*." He got to his feet slowly, fingering a sharp-bladed knife in his pocket while a devious and delightful and horribly evil plan formed swiftly in his mind.

As soon as Pristine disappeared behind the shed, Alonzo darted forward to his car, drawing the knife from his pocket and opening a long and wickedly pointed blade. The right rear tire was worn almost paper thin, and Alonzo drove the point of the knife into the soft rubber on the side, twisting as it went in.

Air whooshed noisily from the tire and Alonzo hurried back to the bench. He was seated there, dipping forefingers into his sack of Mail Pouch when Pristine returned carrying a Mason jar of moonshine dangling from his big right hand.

Alonzo exchanged a dollar bill for the jar and unscrewed the lid, glancing aside at his car as he did so. "I'll be damned," he muttered, "Looks like I got a flat tire there."

Pristine followed his gaze, and both men walked over to look at the flat tire. "Must of just oozed out when I drove up." Alonzo kicked the flat tire moodily. "Tell you what, Pris. I was jest about to say I'd drive you in town to make that delivery. If you'll get the jack outta the back and put on the spare, I'll do it. Me, *I'll* set in the shade and have me a drink of corn likker an' watch you sweat doin' it," he added gleefully.

"I shuah will do that, Mist' Peters," Pristine grinned back at him. "I'll have that ol' tire changed in nothin' flat."

Accordingly, Alonzo sat on the bench in the shade and screwed the lid off the Mason jar and tipped it up and drank from the sweetish liquid inside, and presently he was behind the wheel of the Chevvy and rolling in toward Sunray Beach with Pristine Gaylord seated happily beside him and on the floor of the car, behind the front seat, there was a cardboard carton containing twelve Mason jars of shine destined for customers who had expected delivery the preceding day.

And in the locked trunk of the car was a flat tire and a jack and a lug-wrench, and in Alonzo Peters' mind was the vision of one thousand one-dollar bills fluttering about in front of him, his for the grasping, his for the taking, his to do with as he would.

Alonzo Peters sat very erect, looking from side to side as they entered the town from the west on Main Street, and Pristine stirred uneasily beside him and said, "You best turn to the left next corner, Mist' Peters. Maybe best if I get off there."

Alonzo drove straight on across the intersection and headed toward the center of town. He didn't say anything. He was hunched tightly over the wheel, his face in a concentrated frown. Pristine began to protest again beside him, in a low, hesitant voice, as the Chevvy approached the City Hall and Police headquarters, and Alonzo slowed, seeking a parking space in front.

He swung in sharply, directly in front of City Hall. There, by the grace of God, was Randy Perkins just pulling in to the curb in front of him. Randy Perkins was the grizzled veteran of the Sunray police force who hated niggers and loved to keep them in line. Alonzo jumped out from behind the steering wheel and hurried around the front of the Chevvy to intercept Randy as he got out of his patrol car. He grasped the officer fiercely by the elbow and pulled him around so he confronted Pristine, who still sat in the front seat of the Chevvy.

"You better arrest him quick," he said harshly to Perkins. "I done brung him in, and this is as far as I kin go. I'm turnin' him in," he whispered into the officer's ear, "fer murdering Miz Blake last night. You better stick him in jail while I go inside and claim the thousand dollar *re*ward they're offering fer him."

15

It was almost seven o'clock when Michael Shayne returned from his trip to Moonray Beach down the coast. He drove directly to the motel where he found Rourke waiting for him in his room. The reporter was slouched on the bed with a pint bottle of bourbon open on the table beside him, and a sour expression on his face.

"Heard the big news?" he asked as Shayne came in.

"No. I just drove in."

"They got the guy. That is, *a* guy at least, But he's sure as hell going to be *the* guy before this night is over, whether he is or isn't . . . if you get me."

Shayne sat down with a heavy frown. "Tell me."

"It's a colored boy. Name of Pristine Gaylord. Runs a little still, they say, and lives all alone about twelve miles out of town. He's cut out for the part. Considered a troublemaker and served two sentences for aggravated assault. Neighbor of his brought him in for the reward. A white man that I wouldn't pick over the Negro myself, but he is white. He places Gaylord here in town at midnight. Claims he was driving home from up the coast and passed this colored boy hiking down the road about two miles out of town. He didn't recognize him as he drove past, but he had a flat tire a few minutes later, and this Gaylord comes walking up and he recognized him as a near neighbor and offered him a ride home if he'd change his tire. He says Gaylord acted funny and wouldn't give any explanation for being out there at midnight, except that his car was broken down at home, but he didn't give it much thought until he heard about Mrs. Blake on the radio at four o'clock. That's when the reward offer was broadcast," Rourke interpolated sourly.

"So he drove down to Gaylord's place and offered to bring him into town to make a moonshine delivery, and he drove him straight up to the police station and turned him in. And that's it." Timothy Rourke spread out his hands disgustedly. "I've been around town keeping my ears open, and things are building up fast. They're not saying too much in front of an outsider, but the Red-necks are coming in from the back country, and there's going to be a lynching in this man's town tonight unless somebody does something pretty damned quick."

"What's Gaylord's story?"

"He hasn't *got* any story. He just denies everything. Claims he hasn't been off his place for three days and that

Alonzo Peters . . . that's the white man who brought him in . . . is purely and simply lying about picking him up on the road last night. But I helped shoot that story, damn it. I told you about the eager-beaver young cop with the fingerprinting outfit. I got him and we opened up the trunk of Peter's car and there was a flat tire all right. With the suspect's fingerprints all over the jack and lug wrench . . . fresh enough to've probably been made last night. Which seems to prove Peters' story, and puts the colored boy right here on the scene at the right time."

"How does he explain his fingerprints on the jack?"

"I don't think Jenson's bothered to ask him that. What the hell?" Rourke went on fiercely. "It's his word against a white man's. Who's going to believe a damn word a 'nigger' says when there's a white woman been raped and murdered? It's what they *want*, Mike. You know that. All these Freedom Riders and northern integrationists haven't helped things any. There's going to be a lynching here tonight and there's not one single solitary damned thing either you or I can do to prevent it. I'll have to stay here to cover the story, God help me, but you'd better get the hell out of town, Mike, before things start to boil. There's nothing you can do except to get your head blown off if you try to interfere."

"What's Jenson doing?" demanded Shayne. "Has he asked for help? Troops or the State Police?"

"You know what Chief Ollie Jenson is doing," scoffed Rourke. "He's sitting in his office quaking in his shoes and pretending nothing is going to happen. Damn it! If he gets troops in here or the State Police, he knows some of his neighbors will get shot. They're the people who pay his salary."

Shayne got to his feet slowly, his face set in harsh lines. "It might help if we could produce a substitute suspect." He paused, tugging violently at his left ear-lobe. "I take it you still haven't mentioned Harry Wilsson's fingerprints on that glass to anyone?"

Rourke shook his head. "Leroy Smith knows I've got a set of matching prints, but he doesn't know where I got it or who from. It's not good enough, Mike. Wilsson is well-known and respected here. And all we can do, anyhow, is place him having a drink with her around eight o'clock. At worst, he'll tell the same story he told you. The mob that's forming out there in town doesn't want a white man, Mike. They're getting themselves worked up to kill a 'nigger' tonight, and that's what they're going to do."

Shayne didn't reply for a moment, then he asked incisively, "Do you know where Blake is?"

"I haven't seen him since the chief drove him away from the station to take him to his daughter at the Wilsson house."

Shayne took two paces to the telephone stand and leafed through the thin directory there. He lifted the phone and gave the Wilsson telephone number.

A woman's voice answered and he asked, "Is Marvin Blake there?"

"No, he's not. He was here for awhile with Sissy, but then he wouldn't stay. He's bound and determined he's going to take Sissy away tonight . . . drive her up to Jacksonville where he's got a married sister that'll take care of her, though land's sake knows I told him and told him that Harry and I would love having her stay just as long as she wanted, but he's got his mind made up and you know Marv when he sets his mind to something. So he's over at his house packing up clothes for Sissy to take with her to Jacksonville though I tried to persuade him to let me do it for him. You know, him going back to that empty house where, well . . . who is this calling?"

Shayne hung up without replying. He asked Rourke, "How do I get to the Blake house from here?"

Rourke told him. "Is something up? You want me. . .?"

"I want you to get out and circulate around town," Shayne told him grimly, "and keep your finger on the pulse of things. I *won't* just sit around and let things happen, Tim. You and I may have to make a telephone call to the governor if things get bad."

He went out of the motel room swiftly and followed Rourke's directions for reaching the Blake house.

There was a gleaming, late-model Mercury sedan parked in front of the house when he got there. He pulled up behind it and got out and went up to the front door. He found it ajar, and he pushed it open and walked inside. It was very still inside the house, and a quick glance into the kitchen and sitting room indicated that the lower floor was empty.

Shayne climbed the stairs leading up from the hallway. At the top of the stairs the door on the right was closed, and so was the next door on the left. Another door, beyond that, stood open, and Shayne walked to it and stopped on the threshold.

Marvin Blake sat across from him on the edge of a child's bed that was strewn with an array of dresses and clothing. A suitcase sat open at the foot of the bed, and it appeared to be partially packed with Sissy's things.

Blake sat hunched forward in a miserable posture with both elbows planted on his knees and his down-bent face resting in his hands. It was obvious that he had not heard the detective coming up the stairs, and believed himself alone in the house.

Shayne stood in the doorway and said quietly, "Blake."

Marvin did not appear startled or surprised. He lifted his head slowly and stared dully at the redhead. His face was pasty-white and there were red blotches on his cheeks where his fingers had been pressed. He said, "Oh, it's you," in a dead sort of voice.

Shayne said, "I have to talk to you, Blake. Let's go downstairs."

Marvin turned his head to look at the strewn bed and the suitcase. "I'm packing up here. Sissy's things. I'm going to take her away, you see. I have a sister in Jacksonville." He spoke slowly and laboriously, forming each word with care as though it were terribly important that he make himself understood.

Shayne said patiently, "I know. And I think that's fine. But right now you and I have things to talk about." He stepped across the room to Blake's side and took his arm and pulled him up to his feet. Blake did not resist, but he didn't help much either. He reacted automatically to the authority in Shayne's voice, shuffling along beside him and explaining in a low voice that sounded apologetic, "I don't know what to take for Sissy and what to leave behind. She's got so many clothes. Ellie always looked after that, and now she's not here to do it, and I've got to do the best I can."

Shayne silently shepherded him down the stairs and turned into the neat sitting room where the shades were drawn and it was dim and cool. He urged him toward a chair and helped him to stiffly lower his body into it, and then stepped back and got out a cigarette and lighted it.

He said crisply, "Listen to me, Blake. Pay attention to what I'm saying. Do you know they have a man in jail charged with murdering your wife?"

"Have they?" Marvin Blake showed a spark of interest, though it wasn't strong. "I didn't know that. I haven't talked to anybody. I guess I've been up in Sissy's room a good while. I'd keep looking at her dresses and I couldn't decide. . . ."

"It's a colored man they have in jail," Shayne told him strongly. "They haven't any real evidence against him, Blake. Just that he appears to have been in town last night about the right time. That's all. But they're getting ready to lynch him for your wife's murder. Do you want that, Blake?" Shayne's voice was like a whip-lash. "Do you want another murder in Sunray Beach?"

Marvin Blake looked bewildered. He shook his head slowly, blinking his eyes at the detective's harshly accusing voice. "I don't," he muttered. "Of course not. I don't believe in lynchings."

"Then it's up to us to do something to prevent it," Shayne told him. "Why don't you start out by telling the truth about last night?"

"I have told you. Down at the railroad station."

Shayne shook his head angrily. "I just got back from Moonray Beach where I checked your story. You didn't register at the hotel until just before two o'clock this morning. The evening train from Miami gets there a little before ten."

"I told you I stopped at a restaurant and bar and had some drinks and something to eat."

"And spent four hours there?" Shayne continued to shake his head. "No one saw you, Blake. No one recognized the picture I had of you. I couldn't find a soul in Moonray Beach who saw you last night except the hotel clerk. And he says you weren't drunk at all when you showed up at two o'clock. Also, Blake. . . ." Shayne deliberately made his voice harsh and cold. ". . . there's a train coming *back* from here that stops in Moonray about one-forty. I can prove you were on *that* train, Blake.

"I spent almost an hour on the long distance telephone checking the railroad records," he went on deliberately. "One ticket from Miami to Sunray was taken up on last night's Express. It was the return half of a round-trip ticket. And the train did stop here to let off a passenger. There's a record of it and the conductor remembers it, and he'll identify you as the passenger who got out if I bring him into court. Also, there was one cash fare paid between Sunray and Moonray on that return train last night. You *did* come home last night, Blake. You got off the train at ten-twenty and walked up here to your house without being seen by anyone. Tell me what you found when you got here."

"I . . . I . . . oh, my God!" Marvin Blake buried his face in his hands and moaned like a stricken animal.

"I'll tell you," Shayne said in an unexpectedly gentle voice. "I'll make it easy for you, Blake. You found Harry Wilsson here. Your best friend. He was upstairs in bed with your wife."

"No, no," cried Blake wildly, shaking his head, but keeping his face buried in his hands. "Not Ellie. I swear it wasn't like that."

"But it *was* like that," Shayne told him grimly. "Wilsson admitted it to me. But he didn't know . . . doesn't know yet . . . that you came back unexpectedly last night and caught him here. What did you do, Blake? Hide in the bushes and watch him drive away? Why didn't you jump him then and there? Have it out with him . . . man to man?"

"I couldn't," moaned Marvin frantically, "Don't you see I couldn't? How could I face Ellie if I'd done that? I thought about it," he cried wildly, lifting his face to stare up at Shayne. "I knew I should. I knew I should have come right in the front door and got my gun from the bureau there in the hall and gone upstairs and shot him. And maybe Ellie, too. But how could I? What about Sissy? She'd have to know that her mother . . . don't you see why I couldn't do it? I thought if I'd go away and pretend I didn't know, that it would be all right. And then I thought maybe I'd kill myself instead. That's what I meant to do when I went up to that hotel and got a room. But I was afraid I wouldn't have the nerve to do it and so I bought a bottle of whiskey from the clerk and I drank about half of it straight down and that knocked me out like a light. I didn't wake up until after noon today. And then I thought I'd just get on the train and come on home and no one would ever know I was here last night at all. No one would ever have to know about . . . Ellie and Harry. I thought I could just pretend it never had happened."

"What did you do after you watched Harry drive away from here last night? You came into the house, didn't you, Blake . . .?"

"No, no. I couldn't bear to face Ellie with it. I tried to plan what to do, and that's when I thought about the train going back and how I could get on it and just ride back to Moonray and stay the night there and then catch the Miami train and come on home this afternoon like I was expected to. I swear I didn't even come in the house. I went back down the street away from here, and I remember I got sick about half-way back to the station and I crawled in behind a hedge and was sick and I guess I sort of fainted, and when I came back to my senses fully it was time to go on and get on the train to Moonray."

Shayne was silent for a long moment. Then he said harshly, "You're going to have to tell this story in court, you know. Right now, there's nothing to prove that Ellie was still alive after Harry Wilsson left this house. You and Harry will both have to testify as to what went on here last night."

"Will we have to? What does it matter? Can't we spare

Sissy that? Does she have to go through life knowing that her mother was . . . that she . . .?"

"Don't forget the colored man who's in jail waiting to be lynched for a murder he didn't commit. That's going to happen *tonight*, Blake, unless we do something to stop it.

"You and I are the only two people on earth who know the truth," he went on, lowering his tone and making his voice flat and even so that each word had equal emphasis. "We're the only ones who know about Harry Wilsson and your wife, and about your coming home last night. If I had any proof that Harry didn't kill Ellie . . . that she was still all right when he left the house . . . I might be willing to forget that part of it, just for Sissy's sake."

"Oh, she was!" Marvin grasped wildly at the straw Shayne offered him. "Harry didn't *hurt* her."

"Because she was still alive when you came back to the house and let yourself in with your key and went up to her room, wasn't she?" Shayne asked in a conversational tone. "Was she asleep, Blake? Did she ever know it was you who strangled her?"

"No. Oh, God, *no!* Leave me alone. Can't you leave me alone? I didn't know what I was doing. It's all a blur. And now Sissy will have to know. That her mother is a rotten whore and her father is a murderer. All I could think about today was Sissy. How I could spare her ever knowing."

"All right," said Shayne bleakly. "Keep right on thinking about Sissy. She's the only one that counts now. Sissy and an innocent Negro, who's locked up in jail and due to be lynched tonight, if you don't save him. You owe *both* of them something, Blake. You're done anyway. Sissy has a whole long life to live. Why don't you give her the one gift that's left for you to give your daughter? Faith in both her mother and her father. She's lost them both anyway. There's no way you can change that. But you can give her something to live for . . . something to cling to in the lonely years to come."

"How? How can I?" begged Marvin Blake.

"Help me save that Negro from being lynched first of all. Write out a confession. Here." Shayne found a clean pad of scratch paper beside the telephone and gave it to Blake with his fountain pen. "Make it short," he directed. "Just say, I confess that I murdered my wife and I don't want anyone else blamed for my act. Sign your name to it. Go on, *write*," Shayne ordered sharply as Marvin hesitated. "It's your one chance to give a decent heritage to your daughter. This will never be made public unless it's absolutely necessary. And even then, it doesn't mention your wife and Wilsson."

Shayne stood over him while Blake carefully wrote out the brief confession and signed it, then took it out of his hands and folded it and put it into his pocket.

He turned away, saying, "If this could go down as an unsolved crime, Sissy would never have to know *anything*. Except that her father loved her mother so dearly that he could not stand to go on living after she died. You said something about a gun, didn't you?"

"Yes . . . I . . . ." Marvin Blake's voice became choked. In a moment he was able to continue steadily. "In the right top drawer of that bureau in the hall. It's a souvenir my father brought back from the First World War. I've always kept it cleaned and oiled."

Shayne stepped into the hallway and opened the drawer and looked down somberly at the blued steel of a Colt's .45 automatic. He sighed and nodded, and turned away leaving the drawer open.

He said, "I'll have to go down and see Chief Jenson about that Negro. We'll be back in fifteen or twenty minutes." He went out the front door, closing it carefully behind him, got in his car and drove away swiftly.

16

Chief Ollie Jenson sat alone and frightened in his office at police headquarters morosely regarding the bottle of shine sitting on the desk in front of him. He calculated there were about three drinks left in the bottle if he refrained from gulping.

And it was only about seven-thirty in the evening. With that colored boy locked up in his jail charged with the murder-rape of Ellie Blake, Chief Jenson knew he was going to need a lot more than three drinks to get through the night that lay ahead of him. Then he remembered that Alonzo Peters had said something about driving Pristine in to town to make some likker deliveries and that's how-come he brought him in to jail so easy, so he suddenly figured that the stuff must still be in Peters' car right now; and it sure enough was subject to confiscation, he reckoned, being the property of a jailed suspect and all.

A knock sounded on Chief Jenson's door just as he reached this comforting conclusion to his train of thought. He put the quart bottle back in the bottom right-hand drawer of his desk and closed it. Then he touched the release button on his desk, and the door opened.

Officer Harris poked his head in and reported, "That *de*tective from Miami wants to see you, Chief. Says it's real important."

The chief nodded and settled back with his hands folded over his paunch. "Send him right in, Ralph."

The officer stepped back and opened the door wider and Michael Shayne entered. He said curtly, "They tell me you've got the Blake case all wrapped up, Chief."

Chief Jenson shook his head ponderously and rumbled, "Have a chair, Mr. Shayne. You mean Pristine Gaylord? Well, now, I wouldn't go so far as to say we've got an open and shut case, but I reckon we got enough to hold him all right."

"The way I hear it," said Shayne, "is the only thing you've got is the fact that he was supposed to have been in town about midnight last night."

"That, and the fact that he denies it straight out. Why won't he say what he was doing in town, if he ain't guilty?"

Shayne said, "There might be a lot of reasons, Chief. That's mighty slim evidence to hang a man on."

"Well, I reckon we'll get plenty more before he ever comes up for trial," said Jenson comfortably. "Once we start digging into things. . . ."

Shayne put the palms of his hands flat on the chief's desk and leaned forward to glare at him. "You know that Negro will never come to trial, Chief." The words came out harshly. "You know what's happening out in the streets of this town right now . . . and you know what will happen here tonight, if you don't stop it fast. You'll have a second murder before morning."

"Not so fast now," said Jenson uneasily. "I'm the law here in Sunray Beach. I won't stand for no lynching."

"What are you doing to prevent it?" demanded Shayne bitterly. "Have you called the State Police? Have you asked the governor to send troops?"

"I got no call to do that," Jenson argued doggedly. "May be some hotheads talking lynching around town, but shucks! You know how that is. I guess I can handle things in my town without no outside help."

Shayne said flatly, "You can't, and you know it. What are the chances of getting the prisoner out of your jail and into a safer place?"

"He's staying where he is," Ollie Jenson said stubbornly. "You're from Miami and you don't know people up this way. Mighty fine, law-abiding citizens we got here, I can tell you for a fact. It'd be an insult to them and to my police force was I to admit it wasn't safe for a murder suspect to spend the night right here locked up in the Sunray city jailhouse."

Shayne said grimly, "Suppose you *knew* that colored boy was innocent, Chief? Suppose you had absolute proof that he had nothing to do with the Blake murder? Would you feel just as good about leaving him in jail overnight, if that were the case?"

"If I had any way of knowing that," said Jenson weakly, "I reckon I'd figure he was safer out of town. But shucks, it stands to reason he's plumb guilty. He's got a bad reputation around town, and folks've seen him watching Ellie the way a nigger does a white woman sometimes. You know how them buck niggers get when they want a piece of white stuff real bad."

Shayne said coldly, "I know how a lot of damn-fool southern white men *think* a Negro is about a white woman, but I've never encountered it personally. This is no time to argue that point," he went on harshly. He reached in his pocket and drew out Blake's confession and pushed it across the desk in front of Sunray's Chief of Police. "Read that, and then let's decide how we're going to get your prisoner out of here without getting somebody killed."

Chief Jenson's fat fingers trembled as he unfolded the sheet of paper and read the words that Blake had written under Shayne's direction. All of the color fled from his cheeks and jowls and he looked up at the detective in utter disbelief.

"Where'd you get hold of this?" he managed to say.

"From Marvin Blake about ten minutes ago. I watched him write it out and sign it."

"Not Marv," muttered Jenson brokenly, "He wasn't even here last night. Him and Ellie. . . ."

"He was here last night and he strangled his wife just

as it says there." Shayne spoke slowly and precisely, giving each word space and impact to strike through to Chief Jenson's muddled mind. "He came in on the ten-twenty from Miami and walked up to his house without seeing anyone. He found Harry Wilsson upstairs in bed with his wife. He stayed outside the house until Harry left, and then he went up and strangled her. Then he walked back to the station with his suitcase and caught the one o'clock train back to Moonray where he got off and spent the night."

"Harry Wilsson and . . . and *Ellie*?" Jenson's eyes were round and protruding. "Oh, my God. Poor old Marv. What'll become of Sissy now? That poor little girl . . . knowing that her mama . . . and her daddy. . . ."

Shayne said harshly, "It's a mess any way you cut it. But right now you've got an innocent Negro prisoner to think of. What's going to happen to him?"

"Yeh." Jenson looked across the desk at the detective without seeing him, it seemed to Shayne. The police chief narrowed his eyes to slits and said again, unhappily, "Yeh. Sure does look like Pristine's in the clear, don't it? Soon's word gets around town. . . ." He gestured to the sheet of paper in front of him unhappily. "You say Marv just *give* this to you? Whereabouts is he? Whyn't you bring him in. According to what he wrote here, he's a . . . a . . . ."

"Murderer," Shayne finished for him coldly. "I felt it was up to you to arrest him, Chief. This is your territory, and your case. He's at his own house waiting for you to come and pick him up, I think. I left him there just a few minutes ago."

Chief Jenson said, "Yeh. I guess I . . . got to." He paused and then straightened in his chair and squared his shoulders resolutely, reached down to open the whiskey drawer and lift out the quart bottle of uncolored whiskey.

He set it on the desk in front of him and removed the cork, then pushed the bottle toward the redhead detective from Miami and said politely, "You first, sir."

Shayne reached for the bottle and put it to his mouth. He took a long swallow and his eyes watered. He lowered the bottle from his mouth and ceremoniously wiped the neck of it on his shirt-sleeve, and passed it back across the desk to Jenson. The chief tilted it up to his mouth and gurgled until the bottle was empty. Then he dropped it back into the drawer and got up. He said to Shayne, "I reckon I'll take my car that's parked out back. That way we can come and go without nobody noticing us."

He led the way out of the office and down a corridor to a rear exit where they went out to the chief's sedan parked in the alley.

Shayne sat beside him in silence while Chief Ollie Jenson drove the winding route to the Blake house. It was just after sunset and the cool of dusk was descending on Sunray Beach when he parked his official car behind the Mercury that was still standing in the driveway.

No lights were visible inside the house as they got out and went up to the front door which stood ajar as Shayne had left it not more than twenty minutes before.

The detective held back and allowed the chief to enter in front of him. Jenson paused just over the threshold and switched on a light in the hallway, and he moved forward very slowly to stand over the body of Marvin Blake that lay in front of the bureau with its drawer still standing open, again as Shayne had left it.

The heavy .45 automatic was clutched in Blake's right hand. He had carefully placed the muzzle inside his mouth before pulling the trigger, and the exploding gases had blown most of the top of his head off.

Beside him on the hallway floor was the scratchpad from the sitting room, and written there in precise and unwavering letters, were these words: "May God and my darling daughter Sissy forgive me, but I cannot go on living without my beloved wife." It was carefully signed "Marvin Blake."

Kneeling beside the body and reading the note aloud, Chief Ollie Jenson looked back over his shoulder at the detective from Miami and said thoughtfully, "With just this here farewell note to go by, Sissy could grow up to be sorta proud of her daddy . . . and mama."

17

FAMOUS SLEUTH ADMITS FAILURE

by
Timothy Rourke

For the first time in the memory of this reporter, Miami's best-known and most successful private detective threw in the sponge today and confessed his inability to solve a case of murder.

Michael Shayne, who was privately retained by this newspaper to assist the local authorities at Sunray Beach and to conduct his own private investigation into the brutal rape-murder of Mrs. Marvin Blake two nights ago, stated in an exclusive interview this morning:

"I am withdrawing from the case. It is my conviction that it would be a waste of time and money to carry the investigation further. The murder of Mrs. Blake was apparently unplanned, unpremeditated, and unmotivated. There are no clues pointing to the identity of her killer, and there is nothing in the background of this well-known and highly respected couple which leads me to believe that the solution of the crime will be found in Sunray Beach.

"I found Chief Ollie Jenson and his capable police force extremely cooperative and efficient, and I am satisfied that if a solution to the crime is ever found it will be due to their dogged and persevering efforts rather than to any outside investigative agency."

A tragic aftermath of the brutal crime was the suicide last night of the bereaved husband. The body of Marvin Blake was discovered by Chief Ollie Jenson and Michael Shayne in the hallway of the once-happy home where the devoted couple had lived with their six-year-old daughter, Sissy.

Marvin Blake had taken his life with a bullet from a .45 automatic, a relic of the First World War which had been brought home as a souvenir by Mr. Blake's father. A suicide note lay beside the body.

It said, simply and graphically: *May God and my darling daughter Sissy forgive me, but I cannot go on living without my beloved wife.*

It was signed, *Marvin Blake.*

Mrs. Henrietta J. Jurgen, a married sister of Mr. Blake's, arrived from her home in Jacksonville later in the evening to take charge of fair-haired, orphaned Sissy Blake who was the first to discover her mother's violated corpse in an adjoining bedroom early in the morning after the tragedy occurred at midnight.

Pristine Gaylord, a local suspect who had been held for questioning several hours late yesterday afternoon, was released from custody at eight o'clock last night. Because of the brutal nature of the crime, the indignation of citizens of the community had been running high since news of Gaylord's arrest had spread like wild-fire during the early hours of the evening, and ugly violence might easily have erupted in that peaceful resort area had not Chief Jenson acted promptly and courageously to stamp it out.

Standing on the steps of the City Hall on Main Street and facing an angry group of his fellow-citizens, many of whom were armed and threatening lynch law, Chief Jenson upheld the finest traditions of law enforcement in the South by issuing the following public statement.

"Pristine Gaylord is an innocent man and has been released from custody. Michael Shayne, a private investigator from Miami whose incorruptible reputation is known to most of you, has worked closely with me on this case, and together we have unearthed indisputable evidence that Pristine Gaylord had nothing to do with the murder of Mrs. Blake.

"We have no further suspects at this time, although I solemnly pledge you that this case will never be closed until the perpetrator is brought to justice.

"I now order you to disperse peacefully and go on about your ordinary affairs, leaving the dispensation of justice to the duly constituted authorities."

Chief Jenson's order was obeyed, and by ten o'clock last night the streets of Sunray Beach were as quiet and as empty as on any ordinary week-day night.

At this time the *News* is withdrawing its offer of $1000 reward for the arrest and conviction of Mrs. Blake's murderer. It is convinced that the investigation is in good hands and proceeding in an orderly fashion, and that no good is likely to come from a continuation of the reward offer.

THE END.